CHARLESTON CONUNDRUM

STACY WILDER

Cover design by Brandi Doane McCann
Interior design by Laura Doyle

ISBN 979-8-9854266-1-8 (paperback)
ISBN 979-8-9854266-0-1 (ebook)

www.storystacy.com

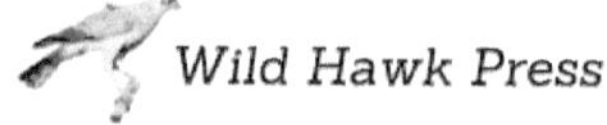 Wild Hawk Press

Prologue

Liz stretched the packing tape over the last box. The movers were due to arrive any minute. Referring to the yellow legal pad, she double-checked her list.

"Stock options cashed—check. Divorce papers finalized with lying, cheating bastard of an ex-husband—check. Atlanta house sold—check. Closed on townhouse in Charleston—check. Signed up for classes to obtain PI license—check." A tear escaped from the corner of her eye. "Damn it, Sawyer," she swore at her ex.

She chewed on the end of her pen and looked around the boxed-up space they once called home. The hardwood floors lovingly restored. The walls painted a soft cream. They'd spent hours picking out the perfect shade. The upstairs bedrooms would never be filled with the children they both had so desperately wanted. Thirty-one and divorced. Not the life she'd imagined a few years ago when she believed in their love. His betrayal still stung. Her blue eyes misted. "No more tears." She brushed off her hands in an attempt to dismiss any lingering memories.

A wet nose nudged her leg. "Hey, Duke." The puppy was a last-minute addition to the trip. One of her co-workers at Coca-Cola couldn't keep him. At six months, he was already fifty pounds of boundless energy. Who could resist an adorable black Lab puppy?

"Dog crate ready for road trip to Charleston—check."

Her cell phone buzzed and she recognized the number. "Hi, Mom."

"Hi, hon. You all packed?"

"Yup."

"Are you sure you want to go? Why don't you come to Florida and spend a few months with Dad and me?"

Liz swallowed hard as tears threatened once again. "Too late. Movers will be here any minute. I'll call you when I get there."

Her parents were convinced she was having a nervous breakdown after the divorce. They couldn't believe she quit her cush job, sold the house, and was moving to Charleston, South Carolina.

"Suck it up," she muttered. Then she perched her petite frame on the built-in window seat and watched for the moving van. She didn't think it was possible to fall in love with a place, but Charleston gave her hope she hadn't felt in a long while. Time for a fresh start. As she tucked a stray blonde hair behind her ear, she recalled the moment she decided to move.

Walking down East Bay, her whole life upended, a soft salty breeze offered some relief from the sweltering heat. She could feel Charleston seeping into her skin. It was as if nothing mattered and everything mattered all in the same breath. The slight scent of hay and horse sweat coming from a nearby carriage beckoned her to rest her feet and take a ride. Facing a pending divorce and a career that kept her busy, yet not satisfied, she was not looking forward to returning to Atlanta. This place enchanted her. Homes, hundreds of years old, were painted the colors of Crayola crayons. The never-ending Southern porches were dotted with wooden swings and wicker rockers. The azalea and camellia bushes were in full bloom and the scent of jasmine collided with the salt air. The clip-clop rhythm of horses' hooves against the weathered street left her longing for a more natural rhythm in her own life. Every one of her senses was engaged; the backs of her thighs sticky with sweat against the hard brown leather carriage seat; the smell of salt, hay, and perspiration; the Caribbean green, periwinkle blue, carnation pink of the houses; the taste of salt as she licked her dry lips; the musical sound of birds singing. She sighed. It had been a long time since she had felt this alive. Perhaps it was time for a permanent change of scenery.

The sound of the moving van approaching her driveway popped her back to the present. Planting a kiss on top of Duke's head, she said, "Charleston, here we come!"

Chapter 1

SIX YEARS LATER

Duke's baritone bark rang in my ears. Sirens screeched. I jerked upright. The neon lights on my bedside clock pulsed four fifty-two. Heart hammering, I emerged from the warm cocoon of blankets atop my four-poster bed. The jolt of cold tile on my feet lifted a portion of the fog created by last night's third glass of wine.

"What's the matter, boy?" Red lights beaconed through the front bay windows. My sixth sense kicked in, and the hairs on my arm responded. I grabbed Duke's leather collar and edged past his ninety-pound muscled body to peer through the beveled glass of my front door.

My stomach dropped. Police cars swarmed my neighbor's house.

My neighbor, Peg, and I had become fast friends shortly after I moved here. Just six hours ago, we'd polished off her stash of merlot. The good stuff … that she'd bought at a charity auction … for three times the normal price.

I couldn't imagine why every emergency crew in Charleston was parked in front of her home. I ran my fingers through my hair in disbelief. "What the hell is going on?"

After slipping into my robe, I left Duke inside and marched toward the red lights and swarm of emergency personnel. Each step felt heavy, and leaden. My gut clenched tighter, and tighter, and I wiped beads of perspiration off the back of my neck. The yellow tape stretched across the sidewalk leading to her front door screamed "crime scene." Streetlamps glowed in the morning mist, and the combination of pulsating red and orange lights gave off an eerie glow. Neighbors trickled from their homes and formed a small crowd. I scanned the faces but couldn't find Peg. Picking up the pace, I headed toward Cassie, the sixty-year-old widow, who lived next door to Peg.

"Cassie, what happened? Where's Peg?"

"I don't know." She shook her head.

My legs trembled, and I had a sinking feeling in my stomach. "What happened?" I repeated. "Why are the cops here?"

"I don't know." Her voice rose a few decibels. "Last night I thought I heard a loud pop, like a firecracker, but I'm not sure. I fell asleep with the television on. Went to the kitchen for a glass of water. Turned off the television and crawled back in bed. The next thing I heard was the sirens."

"What time was that?" The most likely neighbors to have any information were Cassie and Lou, Peg's other neighbor and business partner. Peg and Lou owned an interior design firm.

"Around two," she replied.

I'm not popular with most of the Charleston police force, and that was an understatement. I challenged their good ole' boy club. Even though I owned a Labrador, I operated more like a bulldog. What most of them resented, second to my track record, was my ability to navigate through the Charleston elite. I relied on Peg's friends and connections often.

I dreaded trying to drag information out of the cops.

Matt walked up adjusting his holster. The ginger-colored cowlick he sported on top of his head made him look like he'd just rolled out of bed. Matt was one of the few members of the Charleston police force who was actually friendly toward me. Peg had nicknamed him Howdy Doody.

"Howdy, Liz."

"What happened, Matt? Where's Peg?"

Matt gazed at the ground. "I'm sorry, Liz. She's dead."

That was the last thing I remembered before my world went black.

When I opened my eyes, two EMTs were hovering over me. I had no idea how long I was out. With assistance, I stood, my legs wobbling. The EMTs escorted me to Lou's house, insisting that I lie down on his couch. After checking my vitals, they finally left me alone. My head throbbed. I couldn't believe I'd fainted. It must have been the combination of adrenaline and last night's alcohol. Jeez, I dreaded the ribbing I was bound to receive.

I glanced around Lou's living room and into the dining room. Matt and another cop were seated at the glass dining room table, interviewing my neighbors. Cassie fussed over me with a thick soft cotton washcloth dipped in ice water. She'd appointed herself my official caretaker. Brushing her hand away, I sat up, pulling the blanket tightly around me. I was chilled to the bone even though it was likely eighty degrees outside. The month of May was proving itself hotter than normal.

"How long was I out?"

"Not long. Less than a minute," Cassie responded.

"Is she really dead?" This wasn't happening.

"I'm sorry, Liz. It's true."

"Not Peg." I shook my head in disbelief. She was only thirty-six. She would be thirty-seven in July. Our birthdays were nine months apart to the day.

Lou sat on my other side and draped his arm around me. I turned toward him, staring into his long-lashed blue eyes. "How did she die?" Tears rolled down my cheeks. Aware of the cops looking my way, I gratefully accepted the handful of Kleenex from Cassie, blew my nose, and attempted to compose myself.

Lou rubbed his face with his palms. "Bruce found her. He had the early shift at the hospital and was walking Buddy before work." He paused.

Bruce, a divorced doctor, lived two doors down from me.

Sighing, Lou continued, "Peg's door was wide open. He called for her. When she didn't answer, he went in. He found her laying in a pool of blood. He couldn't help her. She was already gone. The cops said she was shot."

"Murdered?"

Lou nodded.

Shivering, I gripped the blanket tighter in an attempt to get warmer, and hide my robe. Nausea surged. I leaned back on the couch and closed my eyes.

"Honey, you seem awfully pale." Lou placed his hand on my thigh. "You're not going to faint on us again, are you?"

When I didn't reply, he motioned for Cassie. "Will you bring Liz a cup of coffee laced with brandy? The brandy's right next to the coffee pot."

A few minutes later, Cassie handed me a steaming mug of coffee and a plate filled with various types of melon, and a croissant. "You need to eat."

I inhaled the smell of the freshly brewed coffee before tasting it. The caffeine seemed to settle my stomach. I mouthed a thank you, noticing that she remembered to salt the fruit for me. After a few sips of coffee, I ate a couple of pieces of honeydew melon and nibbled on the croissant.

Matt motioned that it was my turn to be questioned. Setting the plate of half-eaten food on the coffee table, I stood, still feeling a bit wobbly. I took a deep breath, attempting to pull myself together as I walked toward the dining room.

Sam, a crusty old cop who resented me for having solved two of his cold cases, snickered. "Have a seat, Lightweight Liz." I grimaced as both cops chuckled, and I prayed the new nickname didn't stick. I wanted to punch back with a snarky comment, but I bit my tongue.

Sam glowered at me from the head of the table. His bald head reflected the light from the chandelier. His bushy brown mustache needed a trim. "Where were you last night?"

"At Peg's house."

Matt and Sam glanced at each other in surprise before Sam continued, "What time was that?" Matt flipped to a new page in his notebook and started to take notes.

"Around seven. Her ex, Alex, had called earlier. She was upset."

Sam rolled his eyes. "About what?"

"He asked her for money to cover his debts. She usually caved, but this time she didn't budge." Leaning forward, I slapped the table. "He threatened to kill her."

"Calm down, Liz." Matt chided.

I pulled the blanket tight over my robe. "Don't tell me to calm down, Matt."

He nodded. "Sorry. Continue."

"Not much else to tell. She hung up on him. She was pretty shook up."

"He ever threatened her before?" Sam resumed control of the questioning.

"He has a temper. He was violent at least once while they were married that I know about. Peg told me it was bad enough that she had bruises. He's not a good drinker."

"What time did you leave?" Sam asked.

"Around ten?" I didn't know why I said that when it was more like midnight, but I didn't correct myself.

"Anything else we should know?"

"I didn't like the situation, so I gave her my old Rossi 38 Special. I told her that I'd had it repaired but I hadn't had a chance to take it to the range to test it. The safety tended to slip," I explained.

Matt pushed back in his chair.

"Go on," Sam said.

"Peg assured me she could handle the weapon. She promised to return it as soon as she purchased a gun of her own and asked me for advice on what type she should get." I gazed at Matt and then Sam. "Why didn't she use it to defend herself?" I asked, incredulous.

"No comment," Sam quickly said before Matt could answer. He handed me a grubby business card. "Call if you think of anything else. And Liz, if you keep fainting, you might want to give up the PI business."

"No chance, Sam."

"Fine. Just remember—this is my investigation."

Chapter 2

Duke's barking woke me up. Again. Cassie shouted my name from the front room. I glanced at my phone, four fifteen. Five missed calls from Cassie. After walking me home, she insisted on staying with me. She agreed to leave after I promised to call her at four o'clock, sharp. I was astounded that I slept so soundly. The throbbing in my head had lessened, but my chest felt like someone had punched me. Hard.

Cassie had a key, so she'd apparently let herself in after I didn't respond. She had a key to Peg's place too. I tucked that tidbit of information away and tried to remember who else had a key to her house.

"I'm fine," I hollered. "I'll be out in a minute."

Cassie stood in the front room with her hands on her hips. Her violet eyes were clouded with concern. Dressed in a purple Namaste T-shirt and yoga pants, she chided me. "I tried to call you five times. I knocked on the door. Rang the doorbell. And still no answer. I let poor Duke out to do his business. I was so worried." She stomped her foot for emphasis. Duke whimpered and put a paw on her leg. "Sorry, Duke." Cassie patted his head.

"I'm sorry. I was sound asleep."

Once she was satisfied that I was alright she left, and I jumped into a steaming hot shower. Letting tears mingle with the water running down my face, I bawled until the shower ran cold. I stepped out, wrapped a towel around my torso, and plopped down at my vanity table. Adjusting the mirror, I applied a heavy layer of foundation attempting to cover my splotchy face. A coat of mascara only emphasized my red eyes. I ran my favorite coral lipstick over my lips. Scary looking, but it would have to do.

Bruce, my neighbor, should be home from work by now. He'd been first on the scene, and I needed to question him. I threw on a pair of jeans and a T-shirt and headed to his place. Duke's walk would just have to wait.

I loved our community, Cooper's Cove, off East Bay, walking distance from Waterfront Park. A horseshoe shaped red-brick street separated two-and-three-story town homes. The meticulously landscaped median was slightly trampled from this morning's crowd. At the entrance of the neighborhood was a small community clubhouse with a fitness center and a pool. All the homes were designed to have a view of the water. Bruce lived two doors down from me and had one of the better views.

I knocked on his front door, half-hoping he wouldn't answer. My emotions were raw, my body felt numb, and I felt like I could cry yet again. I even forgot my notebook.

After several long moments, Bruce answered the door. His clothes were disheveled, and his topaz eyes were red-rimmed. We exchanged an awkward hug.

"Peg. Murdered. This sucks." Bruce ran his hand over his shaved head as if he was trying to wipe the memory away. His ebony skin contrasted sharply with the bright white of his bleached teeth.

I lowered my gaze and wiped my eyes.

"Come on in. Can I get you a drink? I was just about to pop open a beer. It's been a helluva day."

"Sure, I'll have whatever you're having."

"Have a seat. I'll be right back."

Large floor-to-ceiling windows spanned one side of the room framing a panoramic view of the waterfront. The late afternoon sun danced off the gray and black color scheme that dominated the living room. I fingered the stack of *Sports Illustrated* magazines on the coffee table before I settled into the black leather couch facing a big-screen TV.

Buddy, an adorable, friendly pug, bounded into the room. He jumped onto the couch and into my lap. Bruce trailed behind him. He handed me a Heineken and sat down in the recliner. "I hope you don't mind. I let Buddy in."

"Of course not. How are the kids?" I rubbed Buddy's ears avoiding the questions I'd eventually ask.

Bruce had two kids. The oldest, a boy, Tom—maybe nine? The girl, Sheila, was around seven. His ex-wife, Hope, lived in a suburb outside of Charleston.

"They're great. I have them for the month of July this summer. I want to take them to D.C. They should be old enough to enjoy it. Listen, I hate to be rude, but I'm beat. Not only did my day start badly, the emergency room was a zoo today. I know you probably have questions. Can we make it quick?"

"Sure. Of course." I hesitated, not sure where to start. "Tell me about this morning."

Bruce took a long drink of his beer and began, "I took Buddy for a walk before work. Peg's door was wide open. I shouted her name. She didn't answer." He shook his head. "I wasn't sure if it was a break-in, so I ran home, put Buddy inside, and grabbed a baseball bat just in case there was an intruder." He closed his eyes and continued. "I found Peg in a pool of blood. She was in the front hallway, off the kitchen. I thought she was gone, but I checked her pulse just in case. A gun was on the floor. Maybe ten feet away. Her chest was covered in blood. I called 911 and waited until they arrived."

"Did it look like a break-in? Could you tell how many shots had been fired?"

"Whoa, one question at a time." Bruce held up his hand. "Everything else seemed normal. No chairs were overturned. No sign the front door had been kicked in. She was obviously shot. As far as how many times, I don't know. I didn't look for bullets in the walls or furniture. I was focused on Peg."

"Did you notice anything odd or unusual?"

"Other than my gorgeous neighbor dead on the floor?" Bruce asked sarcastically. Shaking his head, he continued, "I'm sorry. Like I said—long day. I saw a broken glass surrounded by water. Peg must have had it in her hand when she was shot. I'm still in shock."

An unwelcome picture popped into my head. Peg's tall body sprawled across the floor; her olive skin and long black hair covered with blood. I shook my head to clear the image from my mind. Taking Bruce's long-day cue, I stood, a bit wobbly, intending to say my goodbyes.

"Are you OK?" Bruce leaped next to me, grabbing my elbow.

"I'm fine. I fainted this morning. It's nothing. Really." I attempted to brush his hand away.

"Let me take a look at you. Sit down."

"Honestly, the EMTs already checked me out."

Bruce pulled a doctor's kit out of the closet and proceeded to take my blood pressure. "Did you hit your head?"

"Barely. My arms took the brunt of the fall." I held up my scraped palms. He parted my hair and pressed on my scalp.

"Ouch!"

"You do have a small bump, Liz. I don't think you have a concussion, but if your vision blurs or you have a persistent headache I want you to call me."

"Sure. I'll take two aspirin and call you in the morning." I stood again to make my way toward the front door.

"No joke." Bruce pointed his index finger at me. "And no aspirin or ibuprofen. Seriously. If you have a concussion that is the last thing you should do. You need lots of rest."

"Call me if you remember anything else?"

"I will—rest," was Bruce's parting shot as he closed and locked the door.

I promised myself I'd rest right after I walked Duke.

***

After our walk, I placed a phone call to Peg's ex, Alex. The call went straight to voicemail. Struggling to keep the anger out of my voice over the threats he'd made to Peg, I left a brief, clipped message. I doubted he would call back, but it was worth a try.

Next, I called my ex-boss and mentor, Gunner. I'd worked for his firm, BridgePoint Investigations, for a couple of years, one of the requirements for getting a PI license. Gunner offered his condolences and apologized for not calling sooner. He pledged to help in any way he could.

I filled him in on what I knew so far, including Alex's threats to Peg. Gunner promised to try to get additional information about the investigation from his contacts at the station. Gunner had served on the force for twenty years before he left to start BridgePoint, and his relationship with the cops was much better than mine. He earned his nickname, Gunner, as an eager young rookie.

My stomach growled, and I realized I hadn't eaten since this morning. I heated some tomato soup and cooked a grilled cheese sandwich, comfort food. Duke happily munched on his premium dry dog food. Turning on the TV, I started transcribing what I could remember from the day into my notebook. Peg's death was plastered all over the news. I watched, mesmerized, for a few minutes, and then finally turned it off, disgusted at the sensationalism. How awful for her family. I needed to call her parents. I was rehearsing what I'd say when my phone buzzed. The universe must have heard me; I recognized the number.

"Liz, it's Liam." His voice was ravaged with grief.

"I'm so sorry about Peg. Please tell Camille too. I should have called y'all already but I didn't want to disturb you."

"It's been a horrible day."

"I can't imagine how hard it must be. What I can do for y'all?"

"That's why I called. I want you to catch the bastard who did this. I trust the cops, but I trust you a lot more. Hell, you're practically family." His voice cracked.

I'd spent many holidays with the Kelleys, and his comment touched me deeply.

"I'm already on it. Whoever killed Peg will pay."

"Thanks." I could hear his sigh of relief on the other end of the phone. "I need to go. It's been a revolving door all day long. Cops, family, friends, reporters."

"Love you. Give my love to Camille too."

I stared at the phone for a few minutes feeling like I'd just picked up a block of concrete and placed it on my back.

I glanced at the time, nine o'clock. I wanted to call it a day, but after the phone call from Liam, I needed to start digging. Maybe my neighbor, Maria, saw something that might help.

Maria, a Hispanic woman in her late forties, and the newest member of our community, had recently relocated from Florida. Her home sat directly across from Peg's. She answered the door after the second knock.

"Am I bothering you too late?"

"No, not at all. Please come in." Maria motioned for me to come inside. "I'm so sorry Liz. I didn't know Peg very well, but I hoped to get to know her better. She seemed like a nice lady. Can I get you a drink?"

"No, thank you. I just wanted to assure you that our community is safe, nothing like this has ever happened before." I'd been inside Maria's home once, and it still had the appearance of someone who just moved in and was getting settled. The walls were bare, and the family room was sparsely furnished.

"I'm not worried. I processed a lot in my years in the Army. This is such a shock." Maria's husband, also Army, died in the Iraq War. I couldn't imagine what she'd been through. She motioned for me to sit down. "I heard you fainted. How are you doing? You guys seemed so close."

I winced at the fainted comment and sighed. "She was my best friend. I'm heartbroken."

Maria absentmindedly rubbed the tattoo on her upper left arm. "I remember when I first moved in. Peg brought me a basket filled with wine, cheese, and other treats. I'd hoped she and Lou could help me decorate this place." A few moments of silence passed as her eyes wandered over the room. "I'm going to grab a bottle of water. Are you sure you don't want anything?"

I shook my head. Maria's welcome basket comment had jolted me back in time. While Maria grabbed her water, I replayed Peg's welcome visit to me when I'd first moved in.

"Come in, I was just unpacking. I could use a break." I led Peg into the kitchen. "Would you like a glass of wine? Is merlot OK?" I cleared a couple of boxes off the island barstools.

"Merlot sounds great."

I poured a glass of wine for each of us and handed one to Peg.

"Where did you move from?" she asked.

Digging into the welcome basket, I pulled out a couple of packages of cheese and a few handfuls of crackers and set them on a plate. "Atlanta. Long story short, my husband dumped me. I quit my job and well, here I am." I was surprised that I was being honest with her so quickly, but something about Peg's demeanor said, your secrets are safe with me.

"Wow. A double whammy. You poor girl. That was very brave of you." Peg spread some cheese on a cracker. "Why Charleston? Is your family here?"

"Nope. Visited and fell in love. I don't know how to explain it … I just felt drawn here."

"Ahh, that's Charleston for you. She's a charmer. Will you go back to work?"

The few people I'd shared my plan with had looked at me as if I was insane. I nibbled on a slice of cheddar cheese before answering. "Well, I've always been interested in law enforcement. I wanted to go to law school but ended up getting married instead." Blushing, I took a big sip of my wine. "I want to make a go at being a private investigator. As soon as I get settled, I'll start studying for my license."

Peg clapped her hands. "Awesome. I'm so envious. I loved Nancy Drew books as a kid." We talked about our favorite detective books, and before we knew it, we'd finished the wine.

Maria's voice brought me back to the present. "Liz, are you alright? You looked like you were somewhere else."

"I'm sorry. Just a sweet memory of Peg." I wiped the moisture from underneath my eyes.

Maria handed me some tissues. "Are you investigating her death?"

"You bet. I won't be able to rest until I know who killed her." I sat up straighter. "Do you mind if I ask you a few questions about last night?"

"Of course not."

"Did you hear or see anything unusual? Any strangers lurking around?"

"I picked up takeout from the Chinese place down the street. Some kids were hanging out. Looked like they were up to no good. Later, I caught up on paperwork while watching a movie." She settled into the chair next to me.

"What do you mean up to no good?" There'd been rumors of drug deals in the neighborhood.

"Nervous. Jittery. Like they were on something. I think they were trying to break into the shop next to WanFu's. They turned away when they saw me stop. Five guys, and a girl, late teens, early twenties. I've seen enough to recognize the signs of drug use."

Charleston had a growing opioid problem. Peg's own nephew, Jackson, had drug troubles. It was incredibly sad to watch the demise the drugs caused. "What else do you remember about that night, Maria?"

"I have trouble sleeping, so I took a sleeping pill. I wear headphones at night for the white noise. When I took the headphones off at zero five hundred this morning, the sirens were blaring."

I switched the subject. "Is the tattoo in honor of your husband?" Maria's upper left arm displayed a red heart framed with blue angel wings.

"No. It's for my brother. He was killed in a car wreck when he was seventeen. A stupid trucker was trying to pass another car on a two-lane road." She shook her head.

"I'm so sorry. How awful for your family."

"Thanks." Maria glanced away for a moment. "When Peg asked me about it, she said she couldn't imagine what she would do without her brothers, and now her brothers will be without her." She sighed. "Life sucks sometimes. You just never know."

We were both silent for a few minutes. I briefly considered a tattoo in Peg's honor. Maybe a hummingbird, her favorite bird. Then I remembered Peg's disdain for tattoos and dismissed the thought.

"Can I ask you a question?" Maria fidgeted with the hem of her T-shirt.

I nodded.

"It's about Bruce. He asked me out last week. I told him I had plans for that night, but I have a feeling he'll ask again. Honestly, I don't know if I'm ready. I wanted to know what you think about him."

"He's a nice guy. Keeps a bit to himself, but he's always friendly when we walk our dogs together. You know he's divorced with two kids, right?"

"Yeah. And I'm not sure about dating a neighbor."

"Why not keep it at a friend's level? You know, go for coffee or a drink and take it slow?"

"Good advice. Thanks, Liz."

I stood. "If you remember anything else about last night, will you please let me know?"

Maria showed me to the door. "Of course."

***

Back home, I sipped on a cup of chamomile tea while I updated my notes. I jumped when the doorbell rang. Duke charged ahead of me. His barking sounded fierce, but I imagined if anyone ever did attempt to break-in, he'd greet them tail wagging. Two cops stood on my front doorstep. I recognized the female, Megan, from a previous case that I'd worked on. I pegged the young male standing behind her as a rookie. His badge was shiny, and he was grinning from ear to ear.

"Do you have more information about Peg? Please, come in. Duke's friendly."

Megan declined for both of them. "It's too early to release any additional information, but we're definitely ruling it a homicide. We're here to remind you that this is our investigation.

And to notify you that Sam said you shouldn't leave the state. Understood?"

What? Were they listening in on my phone conversation with Liam?

"OK … am I a suspect?" I asked puzzled.

"No comment. Just keep out of it and let us do our job."

No way. "Of course," I replied. Better for me if Sam thought I was cooperating. Duke yipped in the background.

Someone once told me that all dogs have super powers. Duke's was communication. He whined when something was up. He yipped when someone wasn't telling the truth. He even howled the words "I love you."

His superpowers often came in handy. Of course, it wasn't too handy when you were the one doing the lying.

Megan nodded and turned, indicating the conversation was over. I closed the door, motioned for Duke to follow, and headed for bed, exhausted.

Chapter 3

Typically, my mornings started with a prayer. This morning I was so mad at God I skipped it. Even though it was barely seven in the morning, I was ready to get to work. I knew from experience that the first forty-eight hours in any investigation were crucial. That knowledge contributed to my stellar track record. I tended to hit the ground running since I didn't have to tackle the procedural red tape.

I had an official office ten blocks away, but I didn't feel like changing out of my pajamas. Instead, I climbed the stairs to my home office. Duke trailed behind me.

My antique white French desk faced a wide window with a view of the water. A wall of white boards and corkboards was hidden behind floor-to-ceiling cream paisley drapes. The opposite wall contained double closets filled with supplies. Setting my cup of hot tea on the coaster, I settled into my gray leather chair and pulled out a stack of index cards from the desk drawer. Duke curled up next to me.

Did the cops honestly believe that I'd butt out of investigating Peg's murder? No way. Not after the phone call from Liam. Despite the ball and chain of grief I was carrying with me, it was time to get busy. Not only did I owe it to Liam; I owed it to Peg.

I wrote down the facts that I knew. She was shot. I knew the approximate time. No sign of a break-in. I tried to remember if she locked the door as I was leaving. I was ninety percent confident there was the click of a lock behind me.

Next, I listed everyone Peg knew. It was a long list. I noted any possible suspects, placing Alex at the top of the list. I broke the list into categories: The people closest to Peg, people with a motive, people with a key to her house, and people most likely to witness recent events. Lou fit into all four categories. I needed to interview people while their minds were fresh, and Lou was an easy place to start. I texted him and invited him over for lunch around noon.

I placed a call to Gunner. He answered the phone immediately. "Yo, Liz, I was just about to call you. Cops cleared Alex. He and his buddies chartered a bus to Myrtle Beach to play poker that night. They left around six and didn't get home until four in the morning."

"That's so wrong. How can they cross him off the list so easily? He threatened her." Duke nudged my free hand. His nose was wet and cold. Rubbing his ear helped calm me down.

"There were plenty of witnesses and security cameras. Be tough for him to pull it off," Gunner replied.

"Are the cops sure he was on the bus trip home?"

"It's worth exploring. I'll do a little more digging. See if I can get any footage from the casino. You working anything else right now?"

"Just a small insurance case."

"Wrap it up quick, cuz you're going to need to focus on Peg's murder." He sighed. "I got bad news."

"How could it get any worse?"

"Hate to be the one to tell you, but probably better if you hear it from me." He cleared his throat before continuing. "The gun that shot Peg was registered in your name. There were three sets of fingerprints on it, including Peg's and yours. So far, the third set hasn't shown up in the system."

My gun? That news hit hard.

"Liz, are you still there?"

"Yeah." I sighed. "I gave her the gun that night for protection. After Alex's threats, I should have stuck around. It's all my fault." I heard a loud noise on the other end, and I knew Gunner had just slapped his hand on his desk, probably frustrated.

"Don't you go down that Catholic guilt trip trap … How many times have I told you that it's your worst enemy? Focus on finding Peg's killer."

Gunner was right. After ending the call, I stared out my office window and watched the whitecaps as they danced across the water. People on sailboats and recreational boats headed out to enjoy a beautiful sunny Sunday. Normally the sight calmed me. Today, I wanted to open the window and scream, "Don't you know Peg just died!"

I took a last sip of now cold tea and turned my attention back on the investigation. Who did the other fingerprints belong to? How could I find out? Pulling my fingerprint kit out of the closet, I decided to help the cops along, starting with Lou.

***

A hot shower helped wash away the shock of the earlier news about my gun. Lou would arrive soon. I needed to prepare for his visit.

Setting a plate of sandwiches and a basket of chips on the driftwood coffee table in my living room, I struck a match and lit my favorite gardenia-scented candle. I hoped the scent would mask any dog smells.

Lou and Peg had decorated this space. My only criteria were that the room needed to be pet-friendly, and it needed to accommodate my collection of ocean paintings. The room was textured hues of blue and gray. The driftwood-framed paintings popped against the light gray walls. Duke's fur balls blended in perfectly with the dark-gray, jute rug. I brushed his dark hairs off the cream-colored pillows on the navy leather couch.

Every time I entered the space I sighed, the stresses of my business fading away. I hated to conduct a murder investigation in here, but Lou would feel comfortable, and comfort was a major factor in getting someone to talk.

Lou knocked and then let himself in. I quickly closed the few feet between us and gave him a bear hug. "What can I get you to drink? Beer? Coke? Tea?"

"I'd love a beer."

"Sit down, Duke's in the back, I didn't want him to raid our lunch."

Lou slid onto the sofa. "Doll, I know you have Duke for protection, but you should be more careful. Keep your door locked. And maybe it's time to get an alarm system. It drove me crazy that Peg didn't have one." He sighed as he smoothed his wavy jet-black hair away from his face. Lou was long and lanky with an angular face that was just plain gorgeous. Too bad he preferred men.

Returning from the kitchen, I set Lou's Dos Equis with a lime twist on the coaster closest to him. "You're right. I've always felt so safe here. I promise to keep the door locked."

Lou grabbed half an egg salad sandwich and took a big bite. "You made my favorite." He munched in silence for a few moments and then asked, "How you doing, sweetie?"

"I've cried more in the past twenty-four hours than I have since my break-up with my ex. I play the last details of our time together over and over in my mind."

"Me too. I'll be thinking about one of our jobs, jotting down ideas to share with Peg, and then I realize she's gone." He attempted to wipe away the stream of tears with his napkin and then started crooning James Taylor's song, "Fire and Rain." Lou was involved in local theater and had an annoying habit of breaking into song, sometimes at the most inappropriate times.

"Lou." I chided him.

"Sorry, doll. You know me. Coping mechanism. What were you saying?"

"When did you last see her?"

"Friday. We were working on the big renovation on Essex Street." Lou smoothed his chinos. "We were having a blast, picking fabrics, shopping antiques online."

"Did she seem distracted?" I scanned his face, watching for any signs of distress.

"Not at all." Lou dabbed his ice-blue eyes with a napkin and blew his nose.

"She didn't mention that Alex called her?"

"No. When did that happen?" He seemed genuinely puzzled.

"That afternoon. And she was very upset. She asked me to come over. She needed to talk."

"Hmm. That must have happened right after I left. So, you were there?" His eyebrows furrowed together as he tilted his head.

"Yeah. I left about midnight. We both had a little too much wine."

"You were there?" Lou repeated, leaning back on the couch. "Doesn't that bother you?"

"Of course, it does." Why did I need to defend myself? The Catholic guilt monster loomed over me. Remembering Gunner's wise words, I didn't explain any further.

Lou hesitated before he continued, "What was the deal with Alex?"

"He wanted money. Again. She said no and asked what happened to all his poker winnings. Probably not her smartest move. He flew off the handle, threatening her. Called her a bitch and every other name in the book. She finally hung up on him." Rattled by this morning's news, I didn't tell Lou that I'd given her my gun.

"He's such a jerk." Lou grumbled.

I pressed on as I nibbled on some chips. "I know Alex and Peg were high school sweethearts, but other than looks what did Peg see in him? I never wanted to ask her, and she never volunteered anything."

Lou took another bite of egg salad. He swallowed and continued. "Believe it or not, he actually has a huge heart. That was part of the attraction. Plus, he was like a god in high school, and she was his goddess. And, the Kelleys and the Thomases—Peg and Alex's marriage was like planned before they were born."

"Huge heart?" I nearly choked on the words. "You gotta be kidding me."

"No lie." Lou crossed his heart. "Then life happened and he became bitter and resentful."

"Why?"

"Football. He loves it with a passion. Was the star quarterback in high school. Everyone idolized him, especially Peg. Then he went from being a big fish in a small pond to a big fish in an ocean. Started as a third-string quarterback at FSU then transferred to special teams. He dreamed of playing for the pros, but he just wasn't big enough. Never got over it, and it doesn't help that Cameron plays for the Broncos."

Cameron was Alex's younger brother. Peg also had a passion for college and NFL football. She loved watching Cameron play. I'd watch with her, but I never understood why people enjoyed watching a bunch of grown men scrambling around hitting each other over a ball made out of pigskin. One of my many traits missing from the typical Southern stereotype.

I set my bare feet up on the coffee table and took a sip of sweet tea. My toes were painted "I'm Not Really a Waitress" red from a visit to Peg's favorite salon two weeks ago.

While Lou munched on his sandwich, I reflected back on that Saturday.

As the massage chairs worked their magic, Peg and I talked about our week. We had some of our best conversations in this salon while our feet were massaged, and our toes were painted every shade of the rainbow. This time Peg chose a mint green called "This Cost me a Mint." I remembered her sharing a recent disagreement she'd had with Lou. Something about some overseas vendor. Apparently, Lou didn't like the arrangement. She vented for at least ten minutes, frustrated that Lou didn't trust her instincts. I mostly nodded and listened. Eventually, we changed the subject to more pressing matters, like which new restaurant we wanted to check out.

Hmm, maybe I should ask Lou about that. "Peg mentioned you guys had a disagreement a couple of weeks ago, what was that about?"

Lou reached for another half sandwich. "You know about the guy in Paris, right?"

"What guy in Paris?"

"The antique dealer, Bjorn. She didn't mention him?" He asked between mouthfuls.

"She mentioned an overseas vendor. Is that Bjorn?" I was completely baffled.

"Hon, they were daaaatttttiiiiinnnggg." Lou made air quotation marks.

"How long?" I asked incredulously.

"Since January. She was totally gaga over the guy. I'm surprised she didn't tell you."

My heart sunk, and I tried to keep my jaw from dropping into my lap. "Why didn't she tell me, Lou?" I could barely keep the hurt out of my voice.

"Damn if I know, doll. I thought she had. Anyway, I didn't like our business arrangement with him. Thought the way we paid him was fishy. Always to the same third party. Peg didn't like hearing my suspicions."

I knew I should ask Lou more questions about Bjorn, but I could barely process what he'd just told me. Peg had a secret lover? "Do you have this Bjorn's contact information? Will you text or email it to me?"

Lou pulled out his phone. "Consider it done."

"Can I come by your offices tomorrow? I'd like to look through the files. Especially the ones related to Bjorn."

"Are you working the case?" Lou rubbed his chin, contemplating the idea. "I guess I'm not surprised."

"Liam called last night and asked me to investigate."

"Oh, my gawd. How are they? I should call them."

"All right, given the circumstances. Is it OK if I come by?" I repeated.

"Sure. I'll be there early tomorrow. I need to start contacting clients. I dread it." Lou stood. "I better go."

"Around ten tomorrow?" I wanted to pay a visit to Alex first.

"That works. Don't forget to lock your door."

"I will. Call or text me if you think of anything else. Love you."

"Love you too, Lizzie."

We air-kissed each other's cheeks and Lou let himself out. While lifting the fingerprint off Lou's empty Dos Equis, I shook my head in disbelief that my supposed best friend failed to mention that the Paris vendor also happened to be her boyfriend. Damn it, Peg.

Chapter 4

After transcribing the notes from my conversation with Lou, I called my parents. I loved them but I was an only child and they could be a little overbearing. Right now, I just needed to hear their voices.

"Hi, Mom."

"Hi Liz. Your Dad's right here. Let me put you on speaker."

"How are you sweetie?" my dad chimed in.

I choked on the words. "Not so good. I have some bad news. My friend, Peg, died."

"Oh honey, I'm so sorry. How can that be? She was so healthy."

I could hear the shock in Mom's voice. I knew they would worry but they would hear it in the news eventually. "I don't know a lot of details, Mom. She was shot in her home two nights ago."

Mom gasped. "Oh my. How terrible. Do they know who did it?"

"Not yet."

"How are you coping?"

"It's rough." I sighed.

"I can't believe you're just now telling us." Her voice rose a note, and I could picture Mom on the other end with a hand on each hip.

"Is the neighborhood safe?" Dad asked. "We can drive up tomorrow."

"Yes. Nothing like this has happened before. The neighbors are all watching out for each other. I promise I'll let you know if I need you. I don't want you guys making the long drive from Florida."

"Promise?" Mom said.

"Yes. I'll call you when I know more," I replied, trying to wrap up the call.

"You're not planning on investigating, are you? You leave this one to the cops, Liz." Dad used that stern voice I remembered from childhood.

Normally, when I shared work stories with my parents, I left out the murder investigations. As far as they were concerned, my job consisted of investigating insurance scams and checking up on cheating spouses. "OK, Dad," I responded crossing my fingers behind my back. "Love you guys."

I paced my living room after the conversation with my parents. I had a long list of people to contact but I couldn't focus. I needed to burn off some steam. Changing into workout clothes, I headed to the community fitness center. It wasn't big, just a couple of treadmills, a few elliptical machines, and several bikes. A handful of floor mats hung from the wall next to a rack stacked with various sizes of free weights.

Expecting to have the place to myself, I was surprised to see longtime residents Linda and her husband, Tony, a recently retired attorney. Linda was constantly redecorating and was one of Peg and Lou's better clients. I waved to Tony and hopped on the treadmill next to Linda.

She pulled her earbuds out of her ears. "I'm so sick about Peg. She and I grew quite close over the years. I know how tight you two were. It must be awful for you." Linda was born and raised in Canada, and her voice had a pleasant Canadian lilt.

"I still can't believe it." I turned the treadmill on starting with an easy pace. "It has everyone on edge."

"We have a security system, but I've never activated it. Never felt like I needed to, but I'm calling the security company tomorrow morning. I wish management would finally fix the cameras and lights up front."

"They better after this." Our management company was great at keeping our neighborhood beautifully landscaped, but when it came to minor repairs like replacing light bulbs, they were notorious for taking forever. "When was the last time you saw Peg?"

"Last Thursday. I can't understand why someone would shoot her. It's horrible."

I shook my head. "Yes, it is." We both kicked our treadmills up another notch. After matching the pace, I continued. "Did you see or hear anything out of the ordinary Friday night?"

"We went out to dinner with some friends. Came home around ten. Had a nightcap and went to bed. Typical Friday. No odd people coming or going. I didn't even hear the sirens. Tony woke me up."

Linda's hearing wasn't the best. I had deliberately chosen a treadmill on the side of her good ear. "What about Tony? Did he notice anything odd?"

She laughed. "Hon, we all know how observant that man is. Are you investigating?"

"Yeah. Peg's dad asked me to." I turned my treadmill up a level to a brisker pace.

"God bless you, love. I can't imagine how difficult that will be."

"Did Tony see Bruce that morning?"

Linda motioned Tony over. "Sweetheart, did you talk to Bruce Saturday morning?"

"He was busy with the cops when I arrived." Tony shrugged. "I haven't seen much of Bruce lately. He's been working a lot."

"Thanks," I said. "If you remember anything else, will you let me know?"

Tony glanced at Linda, then pointed a finger at me. "She working the case?"

We both replied. "Yup."

Linda put her earbuds back in. I turned the treadmill speed up another notch and broke into a light jog.

Post-workout, I returned to my home office and caught up on paperwork, paying bills and invoicing two clients for jobs I'd completed last week. I sketched out my plan for the week and fired off a couple of emails. I felt like I was walking in a fog. Some semblance of a routine helped. Pulling out my index cards, I switched gears. One of the techniques I used when working on a case was to flow chart. For each person of interest, I jotted down a list of questions, and then allowed the answers to take me to yes or no until I reached an end. Sometimes the answers caused me to dig deeper.

I pulled out my previous list of people of interest. Who interacted with Peg the week before her murder? Who had a possible motive? Did they have an alibi for the night of the murder?

Needing answers, I pulled up my background check software, and printed off reports for each person of interest including my neighbors. Perhaps the information would shed some light on possible motives. I placed the printouts in a file folder, and carried them downstairs.

While I ate an early dinner of leftover egg salad, pasta salad, and sliced avocado drenched in chipotle ranch dressing, I reviewed the reports, starting with Peg's ex, Alex. His credit report was a mess. Credit cards with high balances, lots of late payments, but no criminal history. Peg's sister, Chantal, had two arrests for public intoxication involving fines and community service, but no jail time. I was certain the Kelleys' connections influenced that outcome.

Bruce, the doctor, had a temporary suspension of his medical license in Illinois. I wondered why. I skimmed the data on my neighbors Nick and Gwen. Gwen had a history of shoplifting that had stopped shortly before I moved here. Sweet Gwen?

Thumbing through the report on the newest resident, Maria, I discovered additional information on her military background. Completely clean. I didn't realize she'd worked logistics in the Army. Made sense since that was her current job with the shipping company. Cassie had dozens of credit cards, but the balances were low. I wasn't surprised. She liked to shop.

Tony and Linda had a couple of other current addresses that came up under their name in Canada, North Carolina, and Texas. Odd, they never mentioned having other homes. Lou's report contained no surprises. Shoving the reports back in the folder, I silently congratulated myself for knowing more about my neighbors than I ever wanted to know.

Did my newly gained knowledge have any bearing on Peg's murder? Maybe not, but solving a case depended on following one fact to another, no matter how inconsequential the information may appear.

I was listening to Alexa play the Lady Gaga station while loading the dishwasher when the doorbell rang. "Alexa, off." After wiping my hands on a dishtowel, I joined Duke at the front door. Spotting Nick and Gwen through the glass, I grabbed his collar and unlocked the door.

"Nick, Gwen, come in."

At six foot two, Nick towered over me. Thick white hair framed a sun-weathered face. His commanding presence was in sharp contrast to his wife. She was the stereotypical elementary school librarian. Glasses were perched on the end of her nose, and her mousy brown hair was pulled back in a bun. She usually wore a cardigan no matter what the weather. Tonight was no exception, and she sported a soft blue cotton knit dotted with white hearts. I couldn't picture her shoplifting.

"I cooked Frogmore Stew." She handed me an aluminum pan filled with shrimp, sausage, potatoes, and corn.

My mouth watered even though I'd just eaten. "Yum. Thanks. Have a seat."

"Shrimp's fresh off the boat," Nick said in his deep, soothing Southern drawl. I could listen to his voice for hours.

After he retired from Boeing, Nick had started a charter fishing business. He'd taken Peg and me out a couple of times.

"Can I get y'all a drink? A glass of chardonnay, Gwen?"

"Yes. I'll come help you."

"I'll take a whiskey," Nick responded as Gwen and I headed to the kitchen.

I poured a glass of chardonnay and handed it to Gwen.

Her hand shook as she took a sip. "How are you doing, dear? I've been fretting about you. Cassie told me you fainted and hit your head."

"I'm hanging in there. The head is better. The heart not so much."

"It's so awful. I wanted to come over sooner, but I've been afraid to leave the house. Murder … it's so scary. Nick keeps reminding me nothing like this has happened in all the years we've lived here, but it's not helping."

We returned to find Duke on the couch with his paws in Nick's lap. Duke moaned with delight while Nick rubbed his ears.

"Duke. Get down."

"Awe, we were just getting acquainted."

I handed Nick his whiskey. "What? It's been a whole three days since you last saw each other."

Nick adored Duke. He constantly pestered me to let him take Duke hunting, but I always found an excuse and declined. Something about one animal retrieving another dead animal just didn't sit right with me.

"Four days," he corrected. "How are you holding up, Sugar?" Pointing at Gwen, he continued, "This one's been driving me crazy, worrying, and fretting. The only way I got her out of the house was to tell her we needed to bring you food. 'No telling if that girl is eating, Gwen.' That got her attention."

Gwen's eyes filled with tears. "I can't believe Peg's gone." She began to sob. Nick draped his arm around her. Duke scooted closer and put his head in her lap.

Tears welled up in my eyes, too. Grabbing a handful of tissues for myself, I handed the box over to Nick who was obviously uncomfortable with all the female tears.

"What have you heard from the police?" he asked.

Removing her glasses, Gwen wiped her eyes. "I saw they visited you last night."

She was our official neighborhood busybody. Why didn't I think to interview her earlier? My head definitely wasn't right yet.

"They wanted to give me an update," I lied. "They said they're ruling it a homicide. No clear motive or suspects yet."

Duke yipped.

"What's the matter, boy?" Nick massaged Duke's neck.

Thank goodness, Peg had been the only other person who knew about the extent of Duke's superpowers. At first, she didn't believe in Duke's abilities, so we'd structured a series of questions to test him. I wished I could ask Peg a few questions right now with Duke present. Like, why didn't she tell me about Bjorn?

"He's been a little nervous since all of this happened." I deflected the conversation away from Duke. "Gwen, did you notice anything out of the ordinary on Friday?"

She proceeded to give me a run-down of her entire day, starting with breakfast. I should have narrowed the question. My ears perked up when she mentioned Bruce's name.

"I picked up the mail after work. Bruce was knocking on Peg's door. She let him in. He only stayed a few minutes."

"Any idea why he was there?"

Gwen shook her head. "We just waved at each other. I didn't talk to either of them."

She droned on about the rest of her day. "Nick came home around six. We ate dinner. He watched baseball. I read my book in my chair by the front window. It's a great mystery. You'd love it, Liz. I'll loan it to you when I'm done. Tony and Linda came home around ten. I saw you leave Peg's around midnight. Afterward, I went to bed."

Nick was silent as he nursed his whiskey.

"What about you Nick? Did you notice anything odd that night?"

"Nah. Had a few beers with the guys on my last charter. I dozed on and off while watching the game after dinner."

Gwen frowned and continued. "We woke up the next morning to the sound of sirens."

Nick patted Duke's head. "Heard this boy bark, too."

"It was so awful. No one knew what was happening. I couldn't stop shaking," Gwen said.

"Did either of you see Bruce that morning?"

"We didn't talk to him but he was obviously upset. Saw him talking to the cops." Nick patted Gwen's leg. "Hon, we need to go see him, too."

She stifled a big yawn. Nick said, "Time to take my girl home. Call us if you need anything. We all need to watch out for each other."

I gave each of them a huge hug. Heeding Lou's advice, I locked the door after they left. Eventually, I'd ask them more questions, but tonight wasn't the time for it. Maybe later Nick could fill me in on Gwen's past.

After soaking in a hot lavender-scented Epsom salt bath, I crawled into bed. Duke curled up next to me. I was about to fall asleep when my phone pinged with a text from a number I didn't recognize.

Liz, it's Brad.

Brad was Peg's close friend from childhood. He owned a tech company in California and was heart-stopping handsome. My mind conjured up an image from the last time I saw him. His sandy brown hair was tousled and highlighted by the sun. He wore dark blue jeans and a baby blue golf shirt. His toned body fit those jeans well. My heart jumped.

Hi Brad, you in town?

Just got in. Staying with Ian and Irene.

Ian was Peg's older brother by two years. I remembered Brad was close friends with Ian, and his wife, Irene. I texted Brad back.

Give them a big hug from me. This is so unbelievable.

Will do. It's so insane. How can she be dead?

I know. : (

Can I stop by and see you tomorrow night?

What time?

6ish?

That works. See you then.

The last time I'd joined Peg and Brad for dinner, I caught Brad staring at me. When his aquamarine eyes locked with mine, he winked at me. A wink that sent shivers up and down my entire body. I remembered blushing after she told me that Brad thought I was cute. With her gone, I felt like I'd lost my right arm. I wondered if he felt the same way.

Chapter 5

The morning sun streamed through my kitchen window. I was wiping down the countertops when Duke responded with a growl to a loud rap at my front door.

He rarely growled. Typically, he wagged his tail no matter who was knocking. I strode toward the front door. What a surprise—Sam, my favorite cop. Grabbing Duke's collar, I turned the lock and opened the door a crack. "Morning Sam, your buddies already visited the other night. What do you want?"

"You gonna invite me in?" It was seven-thirty. I wanted to be at Alex's office by eight.

"I was just headed out."

"Won't take but a minute."

Opening the door wider, I motioned him in. Duke stood tense by my side.

"You look spiffy," he commented.

I was wearing khaki pants and a white linen shirt. Snakeskin sling-back heels, gold hoops with a gold necklace, completed the outfit.

"You mind putting the pooch up? I ain't too fond of dogs."

Of course, he wasn't a dog person. Sam followed me into the kitchen. I let Duke out onto the back patio.

"Nice place you have here. PI work must pay well."

"Actually this is compliments of my former corporate life and my ex." Not that it was any business of his. "What do you want? I really do need to get going."

"You got any coffee?"

Seriously? I was torn between saying no and curiosity. Maybe he was here to share a development in the investigation. "I'll have to brew a cup."

"Make it black. You're not planning on poking around today are you, Lightweight Liz?"

"No. Your buddies made it clear that I should butt out. I have some errands to run." I gritted my teeth and hit the brew button on the Keurig.

"Good. I need you to come down to the station this afternoon. Four o'clock. Your gun was the murder weapon."

He dropped that last comment like a bombshell, and I gripped the kitchen counter. Hearing Sam say it felt like a punch in the gut.

"And you have no alibi," he added.

I whirled to face him. "Are you arresting me?"

"Not yet." He paused for emphasis. "We need you at the station for further questioning."

"I'll be there. If there's nothing else …" I handed him a Styrofoam cup full of coffee.

"I'm watching you. Stay out of it." Sam grabbed the coffee and headed for the door.

Great. This was going to make my first 'errand' of the day even more challenging.

***

As I drove toward Alex's firm, Lawson and Thomas, I continually glanced in my rearview mirror. My white Volvo convertible wasn't exactly inconspicuous. I couldn't tell if I was being followed. To play it safe, I parked in the public parking garage and walked into the Starbucks across the street. Putting on my Ray-Ban Jackie O-style sunglasses, I prayed I'd blend in with the crowd. Slipping out the rear door by the restrooms, I walked the remaining two blocks, the long way. After ducking in alleys and crossing the street several times, I felt confident I wasn't being followed. I was grateful my shoes had a small heel.

Entering Alex's building from the back, I strolled to the lobby desk and asked for Tracy, his assistant. Alex was a real estate broker and a slick one at that. He'd been involved in several shady developments over the years. Tracy loved Peg and knew where all of his business skeletons were buried. She would get me on Alex's calendar if he wasn't free this morning. Tracy appeared in no time.

"Hey, Liz." Tracy engulfed me in a big hug. "How you holding up?"

"I'm OK." I stepped back. "I love your new haircut."

Tracy's long chestnut brown hair was now a stacked bob, framing her angular face and hazel eyes. Admiring the look, I briefly considered cutting my shoulder-length hair.

"Yeah, I decided it was time for a change." She patted her hair, then frowned. "I'm so sorry about Peg. What can I do for you?"

"I was hoping Alex might have a few moments to spare. I have some questions for him."

"C'mon back. I'll see what I can do."

Tracy pulled up his calendar on her computer. "Looks like he's free for the next two hours."

Alex walked out of the conference room down the hall and headed toward Tracy's desk. Spotting me, he pivoted and headed straight for his office.

Tracy grabbed my hand and we followed, stepping into the large space.

"Alex, Liz is here to talk to you. I saw your calendar was open so I thought now might be a good time." Tracy winked at me.

"Actually, Tracy, it's not. I have work to do. Liz, you can make an appointment like everyone else."

Hello to you, too, Alex, I kept that thought to myself. No reason to start off on the wrong foot.

Tracy slowed her speech down a few paces and offered the ultimate Southern female insult, of which I'm sure Alex had no clue. "Bless your heart, Alex. I know you're such a busy man, but surely you can spare a few minutes to help Liz solve Peg's murder." Bless your heart said with a slight sarcastic lilt was the Southern equivalent of 'you piece of shit'.

"When you put it that way, I'd be an ass to say no."

"He is an ass," Tracy mumbled under her breath.

"Take a seat. I don't have much time, but I'll give you what I can." Alex rubbed his unshaven chin. His ash-blonde hair needed a trim.

"Liz, honey, do you want coffee?" Tracy asked.

"No thanks."

"OK. Stop by and see me before you leave." Tracy sauntered out and closed the door, leaving a slight scent of jasmine in her wake.

I sat down in one of the two chairs in front of Alex's sprawling desk taking in the various Florida State football pictures and pennants on the walls.

"I take it you're investigating Peg's death."

"Yes, Liam asked me to."

Alex pushed back from his desk and crossed his arms. His hazel eyes glared at me. "You know I've already been cleared by the cops? I was at the casino in Myrtle that night. We didn't leave until early the next morning. I have plenty of witnesses, and the security cameras show me entering and leaving."

"Whoa, Alex," I said, holding my hands up in surrender. "Relax. I'm not here to accuse you of murdering Peg. I came to get any information that might help uncover who did."

He uncrossed his arms. "I know you're the one who told the cops I threatened to kill her."

I clenched my fists and tried to keep the anger out of my voice. "Well did you threaten her?"

Alex shrugged. "Yeah. But she knew I didn't mean it. I was just trying to get her to understand how badly I needed the money." He straightened his tie. "Lucky for me the boys loaned me a few grand, and I won enough to pay them back and then some."

Jerk. Another thought I kept to myself. "She was pretty upset by your call. Do you have any idea who might have wanted to kill her?"

"I've thought about it." He leaned forward and placed his elbows on the desk. "Her sister, Chantal, hated her, but she doesn't have the smarts. Then there's Lou. But he's a pussy. He'd never be able to do it himself. I don't know, almost everyone we knew adored Peg. When we were in high school and she was the 'it' girl, she was so nice even the mean girls struggled to be mean to her."

He hesitated and then continued. "She sure ran a lot of money through that foundation of hers. Maybe one of the charities felt snubbed. Or one of the employees was taking money, and Peg found out."

Looking down, he fidgeted with the papers on his desk. "Listen, I know I could be a jerk to her. She didn't deserve it. But I swear, I'd nothing to do with her death."

I was forming a question in my mind about his relationship with Chantal when he abruptly cut the conversation off. "I need to get back to work. You know your way out. Close the door behind you."

"You have a pen?" I asked.

Alex handed me a pen. Grabbing a sticky note from the pad on his desk, I wrote down my number, carefully pocketing the pen in my purse to avoid smudging any prints. "If you decide you want to be more helpful—"

"Yeah, yeah. I'll call you."

I stopped by Tracy's desk on my way out.

"How did it go?"

"Oh, he was his usual charming self." I rolled my eyes.

"I swear if the other partners were like him, I'd be searching for another job. Hard to find one with the same flexibility though. I know the Lawson and Thomas families go way back, and Alex is a decent broker. But I sure wish they'd fire him. He's a snake."

"I wouldn't count on them getting rid of him." I handed her one of my cards. "If you overhear anything that might be helpful, give me a call."

"Of course."

I wasn't satisfied after my visit with Alex. I'd a hard time believing his comment that he had nothing to do with Peg's death. I needed more information. I knew he lived a few blocks away. Maybe I could poke around his place later.

✳✳✳

In Charleston, there's North of Broad Street and South of Broad Street. Peg and Lou's shop was in an old building South of Broad Street, the Chi-Chi side. The sign above the shop said PeggyLou Designs in flowing cursive. Peg never went by Peggy, but the play on Peggy Sue was too much fun for the two of them to resist. The sign said hours were Monday–Friday, ten to three. A buzzer sounded as I turned the knob to enter.

I had met Peg here occasionally when we were decorating my place, but it'd been a while since my last visit. The walls had been re-painted a deep chocolate brown, and there were several new French flavored furniture pieces.

"Helllooooo," I called out, seeing no sign of Lou.

Lou emerged from the back, his eyes puffy and red. He wore a short-sleeved plaid shirt, untucked and wrinkled, paired with indigo jeans. Not his usual dapper self. "Hi, Liz. Tough morning." He ran his fingers through his jet-black hair. "You probably want to get started and I still have a lot of phone calls to make. I turned the computer on for you earlier. Password is PeggyLou. The file room is in the back. When you're done, holler."

Peg's office was huge. I sensed her presence in each detail. The walls were the same chocolate brown as the entry. One corner of the room was anchored by a round mahogany table and six coral and chocolate paisley-covered chairs. The opposite wall had bookshelves lined with decorating books and before-and-after pictures of some of their projects. A comfy chair and ottoman covered in identical paisley fabric were positioned next to the bookshelves. A table and small lamp completed the inviting nook. I could picture Peg in that chair, thumbing through books and sketching ideas for a project. Plants were strategically placed, and watercolors of native South Carolina birds gave the office a homey vibe. The smell of magnolia blossoms emitted from a diffuser. I opened the cream-colored wooden blinds behind her desk and settled into her coral leather wing chair.

I stared at the computer for a few minutes before finding the program where she stored her contacts. Scrolling through, I was impressed by the clientele that she and Lou had built. Not only did they have an impressive list of clients in South Carolina, but they were also beginning to build an international clientele. On the legal pad by her phone, Peg had scribbled a name and number for *Architectural Digest* with a note about a photo shoot. I jotted down the details along with a couple of additional names she'd noted and pulled up their contact information on her computer.

Next, I opened her inbox. Peg had liked to simplify wherever possible. She'd used the same email for both business and personal use. She had another email address for online orders to keep the junk mail to a minimum. I expected her email to be as organized as every other aspect of her life, but it wasn't. The only "filing" system was three separate folders for Business, Charity/Foundation, and Personal. She hadn't done much filing lately. There were over eight thousand emails in her inbox. And close to four hundred hadn't even been opened yet. The deleted folder was empty.

My best bet was to search by name. I started with Alex. I limited the search to her inbox and sent box, and started with the latest. A request for money dated March 5th started sweet and buttery and took a turn when Peg asked why he needed the money. The last reply was puzzling.

> Alex: Been researching the Thomas family genealogy. Found out some information the Kelleys might not want public.

> Peg: Like what?
> Alex: Call me.

The email conversation ended there. What that was about, I wondered. The story went that the Kelleys' and the Thomases' relationship began in the 1800s when they emigrated from Ireland on the same boat. The Kelleys amassed their fortune in the shipping business. The Thomas family owned a sprawling rice plantation. The Thomases' fortune dwindled over time, and they eventually sold out in the late seventies. The plantation was now a historic site and a popular wedding venue. The Kelleys' shipping business was still strong. I'd learned that from Peg, over a few conversations and bottles of wine. I wondered what kind of information Alex thought would be best hidden from the public.

Next, I turned my search to Chantal, which returned half a dozen emails mostly from Peg to Chantal about various family events.

There were hundreds of emails related to Peg's foundation from Jenny, Peg's niece, who ran the foundation's operations. I'd be here all day if I read all of these. The majority of the emails were addressed to someone else with a cc: to Peg.

A couple more searches and then I tried Bjorn.

Whoa. The latest one stunned me.

> My darling Peg,
>
> Already I miss you and long to have your glorious legs wrapped around my body. Our days of love-making are imprinted on my skin. I'm imagining our next encounter and many different ways to bring you pleasure. I pray it is not long before we see each other again.
>
> À Bientôt,
>
> Bjorn

My face felt hot as I blinked back tears. She never even mentioned his name to me. Sighing, I focused back on the search finding a few more emails from Bjorn with similar steamy tones. The few addressed to Lou and Peg were strictly business-related. I turned off the computer.

Lou popped his head in. I wondered if I was still blushing after reading Bjorn's messages. "How you doing?"

"OK. I may have some questions about some of the clients later."

He plopped into one of the coral leather club chairs facing Peg's sprawling desk.

"I need to talk to you." He began chewing on his lower lip. He looked over his shoulder checking to make sure no one else was around, even though it was just the two of us. I sensed a confession was coming that I wasn't sure I was prepared to hear.

"OK … I'm listening."

He hesitated, wringing his hands. "I don't like to talk about it. Before Peg died, I felt like it was all in my past. Now I'm spending sleepless nights wondering if the past will come back to haunt me and ruin the business Peg and I built."

I leaned forward wondering what he would say.

He took a deep breath and continued, "When I was in college, I struggled with being attracted to guys. I was so angry at myself and the world."

"Oh Lou, I can't even imagine."

Lou held up a hand to halt me from continuing. I could tell he needed to get this off his chest.

Staring at the floor he confessed, "I'm so ashamed. I was in a fraternity and I raped a girl."

Shocked, I leaned back in the chair.

"It happened at one of our frat parties. I felt like it would prove that I was a man. She never reported it. There was a lot of alcohol involved. She dropped out of school shortly after that."

Shaking his head, he continued, "One of my fraternity brothers, Kenny, is on the City Council. He knows all the details. I'm worried with Peg's death that it might resurface. I just wanted you to hear it from me and not someone else."

I never dreamed in a million years that this would be Lou's confession. After a few minutes of stunned silence, I excused myself, claiming I needed a bathroom break.

I slumped on the small vanity bench in the bathroom, sickened by his revelation. Lou violent? What I just learned didn't jibe with the man I thought I knew. I searched my memory. Since I met Lou, I could count the number of times he'd been angry on one hand. Never violent. Never explosive. I vowed to pay more attention and notice any signs I may have missed. Sighing deeply, I stepped out and walked down the hall. Peering into Lou's office I said, "How about you show me the file room?"

Lou stood, "You OK?"

I nodded. "Just a lot to take in."

As we walked down the hall past the conference room, he repeated the question. "Are you sure you're alright?"

No, I wasn't alright. I was shaken to my core, but I had to carry on.

"Let's get on with it. If I have more questions, I'll ask."

Lou halted and turned toward me, searching for answers in my eyes. I couldn't give him any. Not now. I glanced away. Sighing, he continued down the hall. "I rarely touched the files. That was more Peg's territory. My job in the back was to keep us up to date with the latest samples and purge the expired samples. There's nothing worse for a client's confidence in us when they fall in love with a fabric you can no longer get." He hesitated for a moment. "Well, I guess there could be worse. I'll leave you to it. Come find me when you're done."

Entering the file room, I noticed racks of fabric samples and two bookcases filled with fabric, wallpaper, countertop, and floor samples. To my right were a copier, shredder, and counter space filled with the typical office necessities.

Opening the drawers below the counter, I found Post-Its, pens, etc. The cupboards were filled with extra paper, printer ink, file folders, and paper towels. The far wall was lined with medium gray file cabinets, three drawers deep, and three cabinets across. On top of each cabinet were two labeled baskets, File and Shred. I peered into the baskets on top of the first filing cabinet. It seemed that someone had recently done the filing and the shredding. I made a note to ask Lou who else did the filing. Surely Peg didn't do it all herself.

Refocusing on the investigation helped ease the shock of Lou's earlier news. I opened the top drawer of the first cabinet. It was filled with client files in alphabetical order. I randomly pulled one out. A signed proposal, project plan, details of supplies used on the project, progress pictures, and notes on the client's preferences. I randomly pulled another. Identical format. I scrolled through the names in each drawer. There was a file for Cassie, another thick file for Tony and Linda, and one for Alex's commercial real estate firm. No clues here. I moved on to the next filing cabinet.

The next group of files contained supplier invoices. I randomly pulled a few of those. Orders on one side and invoices on the other stamped with the date they were paid. Finding one labeled La Maison de Bjorn, I opened it and studied the contents. Several recent purchases – an armoire, a side table, an antique mirror. The file contained pictures and a brief history of each piece. The invoice was puzzling. It was from a company called CM Partners Ltd. I thumbed through the other invoices; all of them were from the same company. The payment instructions stated that the funds were to be wired to a Swiss bank account. I snapped a few pictures. Might be worth checking out.

The baskets on top of the cabinet were empty. Again, it appeared that someone had recently done the filing. The bottom drawer was filled with accordion files containing bank statements. I glanced at the one for last month. The balance in the business account was over a million dollars.

The last filing cabinet was locked. I glanced at my watch. Forty-five minutes had passed. I probably had another forty-five before Lou came in to check on me. If he caught me perusing the supposedly locked cabinet, I could always claim it was already open. I dug through my purse and pulled out my handy picks. It took me a few tries before the lock finally popped open.

The top drawer contained tax returns and legal documents related to the business. Peg had put up most of the upfront capital for the business, and Lou repaid her with his share of the profits over time. The promissory note was marked paid in full. The business was a partnership. Fifty-one percent belonged to

Peg, the other forty-nine percent to Lou. Either partner would inherit the other's interest upon death.

I pulled out last year's tax return. They'd used a local accounting firm to prepare it. I jotted down their name and number. PeggyLou was doing well, turning a profit just shy of two million dollars last year. I pulled out the tax return from the first year of business. Not too bad for a start-up. Loss of $20,000. I made a note to ask Lou about that first year. Lou didn't have the same financial resources as Peg. I wondered how he managed to survive with no profit. By the second year, they turned a profit of $100,000. No doubt, Peg's Charleston connections played a big part in the turn-around.

I closed the drawer and pulled open the next one. I started with a file with documents from her divorce.

The settlement was fairly generous to Alex, considering Peg brought most of the initial assets to the marriage. Hmm, Peg had hired a PI to check out Alex. I recognized the name, Al Thorpe. He was a decent investigator, specializing in domestic cases. Inside the file were several progress reports with details of Alex's gambling and philandering. There were copies of pawnshop receipts where he had sold some of Peg's jewelry and silver. Probably to pay off gambling debts. An envelope contained pictures of Alex kissing a blonde socialite in front of a motel. I recognized her. She'd waved at Peg at a gala we'd attended together. Peg had turned and walked the other way. At the time, I thought it was rude. Now I understood. More pictures of another woman at the same motel. What a piece of work. Disgusted I shoved the file back in the drawer. Even though Peg had shared stories of some of his shenanigans, seeing the details in black-and-white and living color was unnerving.

There were a couple more files containing deeds to various assets Peg owned. I jotted down addresses of any real estate. More files with statements from her investment accounts. I knew her financial adviser. She managed my money too. In fact, Peg had introduced me to her.

I closed that file drawer and opened up the last one. The drawer was filled with Peg's personal bank statements, organized by month. I pulled out the March folder. Sure enough, there was a copy of the check written to Alex dated March 5th for ten thousand dollars. I made a quick copy of the page and shoved it in my purse. I wanted a physical copy to present to Alex. I couldn't wait to see his reaction.

After thumbing through a couple more folders, I locked the cabinet just as Lou walked in. Making a show of looking in the baskets on top, I prayed he hadn't seen my sleight of the hand with the lock.

"Hey Liz, are you hungry? I'm beat and starving. I was thinking about grabbing a burger."

I glanced at my phone. "I can't believe it's two o'clock. That sounds great. I'll wash up and meet you out front."

Chapter 6

While washing my hands, I wondered if I could eat lunch with Lou after his confession, but I needed to ask follow-up questions about the day's discoveries. And despite it all, I was hungry.

On the short walk over to Burgers and Buns, Lou asked, "Are we OK?"

I gave him a slight nod.

"I want you to know that I went through a lot of therapy after that happened. I never told the therapist any details about that night, but she helped me come to terms with being gay."

His explanation helped ease the knots in my stomach. Entering the restaurant, we walked to the counter and placed our orders. We agreed to split an order of their famous onion rings. My mouth was already watering. I'd have to hit the gym to make up for this lunch. I filled a glass with unsweetened tea and a splash of sweet tea and joined Lou at a picnic table by the window. Covered with red-and-white checkered cloths, each table had a basket with condiments and paper towels. I set the number for our order on the table.

"How'd it go, Liz? What did you find?"

"I have a lot of names and numbers and people to follow up with. A lot of questions and not many answers. Mind if I ask you a few?"

"Shoot."

"Tell me about your clients. And how you and Peg built the business. I've never heard any stories of the early days."

"We literally started the business on the back of a napkin. We were at our five-year high school reunion. Peg and Alex had been married about a year, but Alex had no interest in attending. So, Peg and I went together. I'd just 'come out.'" Lou formed quotation marks with his hands.

"We stayed for a couple of hours catching up with former classmates and then went to the Francis Marion Hotel for a drink," he went on. "We sat there gossiping about our classmates and by the second martini, the conversation shifted to our professions. Peg was freelancing, doing occasional design jobs for friends and family. I was working for the furniture chain, Fab Furniture, and was bored to tears."

I nodded as he continued. "We started fantasizing about ways we could redo the hotel and it was amazing how our ideas just clicked together. Then Peg was like—we could do this Lou. I jokingly said, 'Yeah, we could call it PeggyLou.' Peg jumped out of her chair and said 'I love it.' We started jotting down everything we would need to do, and the rest is history. The hotel was one of our first clients."

I remembered seeing the name in the files. "How did you make it? The first year had to be tough."

Just then, our order arrived. I'd ordered the 'Cue Burger, medium well. A juicy barbequed hamburger on a whole-wheat bun covered in barbeque sauce with red onion and pickles. I added a couple of onion rings to my plate and covered them with a generous sprinkling of salt. Lou had chosen the Shroom Burger, a hamburger on a pretzel bun drenched in sautéed mushrooms and pepper jack cheese. We sat silent for several minutes savoring our meals before the conversation resumed.

Lou wiped his mouth and gulped down some water before continuing. "When I left the furniture company, I received a bit of a settlement. My boss was homophobic and hadn't treated me well. In fact, it was outright discrimination. I went to HR. They did an investigation, and the company was happy to make the whole thing go away. The first year and a half were tight, though. I borrowed money from Peg, but I always paid her back." Lou's blue eyes misted over with the memories.

"What about your clients? Were there any angry clients? Any strange clients?" I took a bite of hamburger, careful to keep the barbeque sauce from dripping onto my white linen shirt.

"Angry?" He paused to think for a moment. "Maybe early on we had one or two where the project didn't go quite like we planned. Or better said, we didn't spend enough time in the planning phase to get to the bottom of what the client wanted and needed. Sometimes you have to read between the lines. Over the past two years, we've referred a couple of people to other decorators, claiming we were too busy to accommodate them. After a while, it's easy to spot the difficult ones. As far as strange, this is Charleston, honey. We've had our fair share of strange."

"Like what?"

"Like the woman who insisted we do her bedroom in shades of purple with a mirrored ceiling. Or the couple who wanted us to find a stuffed peacock for their living room?" He chuckled. "Oh, I almost forgot about Barbie."

"Hush your mouth. You seriously have a client named Barbie?"

"Well, had. She was a piece of work. Third trophy wife to the infamous Marcus Miller." Ah, Marcus Miller, the man who owned several successful car dealerships and constantly advertised on local TV.

"Barbie was determined to get their home in *Architectural Digest*. She thought we were her golden ticket. She constantly changed her mind, and she wanted everything yesterday. Peg finally told her the arrangement wasn't a good fit and recommended several other decorators. Barbie was furious and tried to throw her status around to discredit our business."

"New money versus old money. I bet she got nowhere. When was that?"

"About a year ago."

I made a mental note to follow up with Barbie. "I noticed that you never paid Bjorn's antique business directly. Is that typical?"

"No. I told you … something was fishy about the whole arrangement."

"Do you know anything about the organization that you sent the funds to?"

"Apparently Bjorn's uncle is a partner in the company. I asked Bjorn about it once, and he gave me some vague answer."

"What did Peg think?"

"Like I said the one time I brought the subject up, she had a fit. We didn't discuss it after that."

I changed the direction of the conversation. "Who else does the filing? Everything's so organized."

"Peg used students from the Art Institute. She liked to introduce them to the business side of decorating. She was meticulous about everything being set up a certain way. I was officially banned from doing the filing. If I pulled a document, I wasn't even allowed to put it away. It had to go in the basket on top. I don't know how I'm going to manage without Peg."

A tear ran down Lou's cheek, and I gave him a moment to compose himself. "What will you do with the business?"

"Continue on for now. Maybe bring in more help?" Lou shook his head and sighed. "But how can it be PeggyLou without Peg?"

We stood and tossed the few remnants of our meal into the trash, placing the plastic trays and baskets on top of the waste bin. It was three-thirty. I was due at the police station in thirty minutes. I placed a quick call to Cassie and asked her to let Duke out back. I hoped to make it up to him with a long walk before Brad arrived.

***

I arrived at the station around ten after four. Sam was waiting for me at the front desk.

"You're late."

I shrugged. "Traffic." After signing in at the reception desk, I followed him down the hall to a conference room where Matt was already seated.

"Hi, Liz. Would you like a drink? Coffee? Water?" You'd think Sam would offer since I'd given him coffee this morning. At least Matt had some manners.

"No thanks. Let's get started."

Sam proceeded to the head of the table and dropped into his seat with a thud. The man could stand to lose at least forty pounds. He tapped his fingers on the table. "When's the last time you cleaned that gun of yours?"

"Right after I picked it up from the shop. The week before I gave it to Peg." The shop had also cleaned the gun but I was a stickler for a spotless weapon.

"Anyone else touch it before you gave it to Peg?"

That confirmed what Gunner told me. There was another set of prints on the gun. "No. I handed Peg the gun right after that." I

58

wondered if I should share the prints I lifted from Lou and Alex. And then there was the bank statement burning a hole in my purse. Although passing the information on would be proof that I wasn't butting out of the case. Maybe better to do some more digging and fill them in when I had something more concrete.

"You and Peg ever have any arguments?"

"All friends argue."

Sam shifted his weight in the chair. "Be more specific."

"OK. We had disagreements, but only one big argument. It was a couple of years ago." I shuddered as I described how Peg and I had engaged in a shouting match about a guy she was dating. His ex-wife was one of my clients. I'd gathered evidence that proved the scumbag was cheating on her, with more than one woman. Peg hadn't liked hearing it and didn't talk to me for a week.

Sam rubbed his chin. "Seems your neighbor saw you leave Peg's around midnight that night. You told us ten."

I should've known that would come back to bite me. "I hit my head on the ground. I wasn't one hundred percent when you questioned me. It actually was closer to midnight when I left."

"Oh yeah. Nearly forgot we're dealing with Lightweight Liz, Matt. Any other reason for the slip-up?"

"No."

Sam leaned forward. "You go back there that night?"

I shook my head. "I'd had a little too much wine. Crawled into bed and was out within minutes. I didn't even hear the sirens. Duke's barking woke me up."

"You got a key to her house?"

"Yes."

"Anyone else got a key?"

"Her parents." I reflected back on my notes. "For sure, Lou and Cassie. Possibly Gwen?"

"Jeez, you folks all have keys to each other's places?"

I shrugged. The question didn't deserve an answer.

"Duke bark at all during the night?" Sam continued.

"If he did, I didn't hear it. He was curled up in the bed with me all night." Maybe Sam was sharper than I thought.

"Seem strange to you he didn't bark?"

I thought about it for a few seconds. "Maybe whoever it was entered from the back? I'm not sure he would've heard that. Or maybe the entry wasn't forced?" I was puzzled.

"Anything else you left out or forgot to tell us?"

"Nope." I glanced at my watch. It was four-thirty. "Are we finished?"

"Just remember—"

"It's your investigation. And I'll call you if I think of anything." I finished for him. "Bye Slowpoke Sam," I mumbled under my breath.

Matt stood up. "I'll walk you out."

After escorting me to my car, he said, "Liz, between you and me, Sam is focused on you as the primary suspect. He's struggling with motive though." Matt scuffed his right shoe back and forth on the concrete parking lot. "I just thought you should know."

"Thanks, Matt." Seriously, Sam? Rule number one—never jump to a conclusion too early in a case. I thought about sharing the highlights of what I'd learned so far with Matt, but my gut instinct caused me to hesitate. Nope, he'd just confirmed the wisdom of my decision to keep what I had to myself. The urgency to solve Peg's murder had just intensified, and the cops were not on my side.

***

Brad showed up at six p.m. sharp. Hanging on to Duke's collar, I opened the door and motioned him inside. As soon as I let Duke go, he did his usual, "Oh, you are my new best friend", meet and greet.

"Sorry, I hope you like dogs."

"Are you kidding, I love Labradors. Had a couple growing up." Brad bent down and scratched Duke's back and massaged his ears. "I'd love to have one except I travel too much."

He stepped around Duke and enfolded me in a hug that set my hormones hopping, which seemed so inappropriate. His body felt tight, and he seemed on edge. I inhaled his scent. He smelled like freshly washed sheets set outside to dry in the sun.

I stepped back, putting a safe distance between us. "You look tired."

Brad ran his hand through his sandy brown hair, "Yeah. Haven't been sleeping well. Plus the time change."

"Have a seat. What can I get you to drink?"

"You have any scotch?" Brad rubbed his faded jeans with his hands and sat down on the couch. His white polo shirt contrasted with his California tan. His hair was slightly tousled. The sleeves of his shirt stretched tight over well-developed biceps. He looked amazing.

"Sure do." I resisted peering into his red-rimmed aquamarine eyes.

"With ice and a splash of water."

"Be right back." In the kitchen, I fixed his drink and poured a glass of malbec for myself.

Handing Brad his scotch, I sat in the chair next to the couch. Duke wedged his way between the couch and the chair demanding to be petted. "How are you? How are Ian and Irene?" I asked.

"Getting by. The house is pretty chaotic. Neighbors dropping casseroles off. Family coming in and out, trying to sort out all the funeral details and everything else. How are you?" Brad emphasized the word you.

"Hanging in there. I miss Peg like crazy." I sighed. "I need to go see Liam and Camille."

"Liam said you're investigating?"

"Yeah. I'd do it anyway, but when he asked, there was no way I'd say no."

Brad was silent for a minute, and I could sense the emotion building inside him. His hands clenched the sofa cushion and his Adam's apple was bobbing up and down. Duke gave a small whimper. I chewed on my lower lip as I waited for him to continue.

"Any progress?"

"Some," I was deliberately vague.

"Some? That's all you have? Seriously, Liz?" He stood up and started pacing.

"What have you done so far?" he demanded.

I was taken aback at the sudden turn in tone. I didn't know what to say.

The volume of Brad's voice increased a few decibels. "Liz, what kind of progress have you made?" He raised both arms to emphasize the question.

Duke started whining which caught Brad's attention, "Sorry, boy."

Finally, I found my voice. "Listen, Brad, you're not my client. And I'm not one of your employees. I can't give you information I haven't shared with Liam yet. But if you sit down, I will tell you what I can."

Brad remained standing for a few moments before finally settling back on the sofa. He reached for his glass and took a gulp of scotch. After a few minutes of silence, the tension eased. He let out a big sigh, "I'm sorry … It's just … well … I can't believe she was murdered." He put his head in his hands. Duke hopped up on the couch next to him nudging his hand with his wet nose.

I grabbed some Kleenex and sat down on the other side placing my hand on Brad's thigh trying to offer some comfort while tears streamed down my face. After a few moments, I stood. "I'll give you a few minutes."

Secure in the kitchen, I topped off my wine. I needed some time, too. Brad's anguish connected with mine, tugging at my heartstrings. Yet despite it all, I couldn't help noticing the firmness of his thigh, which again seemed so out of place. I turned my face upwards and said a silent prayer, asking God for help with the whole mess.

When I returned to the living room, Brad was massaging Duke's ears. He looked spent. "I'm sorry, Liz."

"No need to apologize. It's tough. We both miss her." I sat down and proceeded to tell Brad what I could. Then I said, "If you don't mind, there are a few questions I'd like to ask."

"Sure. Whatever I can do to help."

"When did you last talk to Peg?"

"Anytime I made a donation, she'd send me a thank you email along with a proposed time to FaceTime. It was our weird way of ensuring we stayed in touch despite distance and busy schedules. Usually, we blocked off a full hour and often chatted longer. I talked to her about two and a half weeks ago."

"What about?" I asked.

"Work, the latest news around our friends and her family. Chantal was a big source of frustration for her. Peg told me she thought the drinking was getting worse." He took a sip of scotch and then continued. "Talked about my training for the upcoming triathlon … oh also the latest on the foundation and the summer gala."

"Did she ever mention a guy named Bjorn?"

"Yeah. We talked about him too. Peg said he was a lot of fun and made her Paris trips more exciting. She was enjoying herself. She wanted me to meet him and give my opinion."

I blushed slightly remembering the emails from Bjorn to Peg. "You know, Brad, she never told me she was dating that guy. I can't understand why."

"Hon, Peg was funny like that. She was always trying to protect other people's feelings. I'm sure she wanted to tell you."

"What feelings did she need to protect around me?" I asked totally confused.

"I dunno. Maybe she felt bad that she found someone. And you … well…" He gave a slight shrug. "I know she cared a lot about the friendship you shared." He offered a half-grin.

The implied 'she felt bad that she found someone while I hadn't' stung. Did everyone but me know about Bjorn? Why didn't she tell me?

Brad glanced at his Fitbit. "I promised Ian and Irene I'd be back by seven for dinner. Should I call them and let them know I'll be late?"

"No. That's OK. We can talk later if I have more questions."

I walked him to the door. We hugged and then he kissed the top of my head, which sent tingles down to my toes.

"Guess I'll see you at the funeral on Thursday."

My heart sank. I'd been so busy trying to solve the murder; I nearly forgot Thursday was the service. Or maybe I just wanted to pretend that all of this wasn't real.

Not two minutes after Brad left, my phone buzzed. I recognized the first six digits. The police station.

"This is Liz."

"Is this Lightweight Liz?"

"Funny, Sam. What do you want?"

"I have more questions for you. Be down to the station eight a.m. sharp tomorrow."

He hung up without giving me a chance to respond. This was starting to feel like harassment. "Grrr," I hissed through gritted teeth. Sure thing Sam, I'll be there at eight. Southern time.

I wondered if I should have a lawyer present.

Chapter 7

After my second visit to the police station, I was convinced Sam had made little progress, if any, finding Peg's killer. He asked a few more questions about Alex and some questions about Cassie. The questions didn't make any sense. Had the interview been his weird way of keeping tabs on me? Frustrated, I picked up Duke from home, and we walked the ten blocks to my official office. I needed to put in a couple of concentrated hours of work.

My office sat above a gift shop on King Street, North of Broad, the non-Chi-Chi side of Charleston. The stairs were somewhat steep and narrow, but I loved the old red-brick building and the original wood floors. Most of the time, I worked from home, but occasionally I needed space to meet a client or simply a change of scenery. Six office spaces of varying sizes were housed on the second floor. All leased. A third floor contained additional office space occupied by a small engineering firm. My office was the first one to the left with a view of King Street. Next to me was a new tenant, Carol James, an insurance agent. The rest of the tenants on my floor had been here as long as I had, or longer - a lawyer, a psychologist, an accountant, and a small marketing firm. We didn't socialize much, but we did share a common kitchen and often had gatherings for holidays.

My office, the smallest one on the floor, had just enough space for a desk, an ergonomically correct chair, a couple of chairs for clients, and a dog bed for Duke. The door was polished pine with my name on a removable brass plate. Peg had begged to redo the room, but I didn't see the point. The only artwork was a framed copy of my PI license. One wall was exposed red-brick; the other was painted with special paint so I could use it as a whiteboard. Some of the tenants had glass fronts to make up for not having a window. Instead, I had a wall covered with cork to pin index cards, pictures, and whatever else might visually help with a case. When I was working multiple cases at once, it was how I kept track. Right now, Peg's murder and a small insurance investigation were the only items on the docket. In the front corner, Duke curled up in his bed with a couple of his favorite toys.

Gunner called as soon as I settled in. "Preliminary autopsy results are in. Word is they're releasing the body to the funeral home tonight."

Wincing at the word body, I asked, "So, what's the verdict?"

"Nothing we didn't already know. Officially it's a homicide. Cause of death a single gunshot wound to the chest. If it's any consolation, she didn't suffer long."

"That was a quick turn-around on the autopsy."

"Peg's dad pulled some strings with the ME. Guess they went to school together. Gotta run. Take care kid."

Time to get to work. I pulled index cards out of my oversized Louis Vuitton tote and started pinning them to the corkboard. Standing back, I rearranged a couple and repeated until I was satisfied. On the neighboring wall, I wrote down pertinent details, estimated time of death, method of death, possible suspects, potential motives, and alibis.

- Alex, Peg's ex—motive: anger/revenge, has an alibi.
- Bjorn, Peg's boyfriend, PeggyLou supplier—motive unclear, alibi?
- Barbie, the scorned client—motive: anger/revenge, alibi?
- Bruce, Peg's neighbor, first to arrive on the scene— motive unclear, alibi?
- Chantal, Peg's sister—motive money: possibly jealousy? alibi?
- Jenny, Peg's niece, and the foundation's operations director—motive money? alibi?
- Lou, Peg's friend, neighbor, and business partner, motive: money—stands to inherit the business, no alibi.

As I read over the list, I realized that the first thing I needed to do was uncover what most of them were doing the night of Peg's murder. I walked back to the index cards jotting down additional details. Back to the whiteboard wall, I listed my questions. At the top of the list was: How did the killer gain entry? Peg would have opened the door to most of them except maybe Alex and Barbie.

Next: What was the family secret? I was puzzled how that would fit, but it was a question demanding an answer.

And then: Why was Bjorn so specific about payment instructions? I made a side note to follow up on Bjorn's business.

Even though he had an alibi, Alex was still at the top of my suspect list. I wasn't convinced the alibi was airtight. There was also the possibility that he'd hired someone. Still, despite the fact that Alex was suspect number one, I wasn't about to make the same mistake Sam did and jump to conclusions. Facts matter.

And I still had a lot of fact-finding in front of me.

Next, I transcribed the list of additional people from my note cards; people close to Peg and those who may have helpful information. I stepped back and studied the wall rubbing my chin. The list of people was long, and I knew I'd be adding more as the investigation unfolded. I needed to prioritize.

Most of my work was more mundane—theft, cheating spouses, fraud, etc. However, murder wasn't a new one for me. Over time, I'd perfected a technique that helped me solve a handful of murder cases, including a few cold cases that had remained mysteries for years. After working the inner circle of key suspects, I then fanned out to the other players, returning to the key suspects when armed with more information. Suspects often became flustered and panicked when inconsistent responses caught up with them.

I sat down at my desk and fired up my computer. Opening up my report template, I typed in the basics of the case. I doubted I'd be delivering Liam a formal report, but I owed him an update. Writing the report would help me get my thoughts straight before calling him. Satisfied, I hit the save button and placed a call to Liam. It went to voice mail, so I left a message asking if I could come to visit them this afternoon.

Rolling my head from side to side, I tried to ease some of the tension in my neck. I peered out the office window. The sidewalks were overflowing with tourists and locals. It was easy to tell them apart. The tourists wore screen-printed T-shirts, jeans or shorts, baseball caps or visors, and flip flops or tennis shoes, depending on the season. The locals, more smartly dressed, were usually in no hurry to get anywhere fast. Steam rose off the street. I wiped droplets of condensation from the left edge of the window. Another humid day.

I glanced at my watch. It was past noon. I pulled out my phone and took a picture of the whiteboard. Packing up the index cards, I secured them with a rubber band and dropped them in my tote. "C'mon Duke." I snapped his leash to his collar, and we headed out for lunch.

Turning down the sidewalk, we walked toward Southern Charm, my favorite teashop. The owner greeted me at the door.

"Hey Ellie, how are you?"

"Can't complain. Hey there, Duke." Ellie reached down and patted Duke's head. Standing back up, she placed her hand on my arm and said, "I'm so sorry about Peg."

Ellie's wrinkled face, framed by white chin-length hair, radiated compassion. It was almost too much to bear.

"I still can't believe she's gone." My eyes misted over.

"I can't imagine how difficult this must be for you."

I nodded, then my stomach grumbled, and we both chuckled.

Ellie released my arm. "Sounds like you're hungry."

"I am." I studied the chalkboard advertising the daily special. "I'll take the special and an iced tea."

Duke and I sauntered to my usual table on the back patio that had a view of the street. I people-watched while I waited for my food. Duke curled up by my chair. My phone pinged with a text from Liam.

> Hi Liz. Got your VM. Camille and I are meeting with
> the priest at 1. Meet us at the church after?
>> Sure. What time?
> Does 2 work?
>> See you then.

Ellie arrived with my lunch. The smell of cream of mushroom soup, ranch-drenched salad, and scones reminded me of just how hungry I was. She set a bowl of water next to Duke and then placed two iced teas on the table before pulling up a chair.

"This mushroom soup gets better each time I try it." I sniffed a spoonful trying to place the herbs. They were a lovely compliment to the earthiness of the fresh mushrooms and the sweetness of the cream.

"Thanks. I've been experimenting with my herb garden." She placed her hand on top of mine. "Honey, I know you're hurting. I can't even imagine how much. I just want you to know that I'm here anytime you need to talk."

"I appreciate that," I replied. We sat in silence for a few minutes. "I'll be alright."

"I should get back to the kitchen. Holler if you need…well… anything. And honey, this one's on the house."

After lunch, I dropped Duke off at home, and headed to the church to meet Liam and Camille. I arrived at St. Michael's twenty minutes early. Entering the Adoration Chapel, I sat in the last pew and lowered the kneeler. My faith had hit a crisis point after my split with my ex, Sawyer, and I didn't want to revisit that darkness. My old high school guidance counselor had helped me pull through and out the other side. Her gentle counsel had given me the courage to move to Charleston and follow my dreams of becoming a PI.

Look where that landed me. I bit my tongue to prevent a flow of cuss words. My best friend was dead, and I was investigating her murder. I dreaded telling her parents that my gun was the murder weapon. Really, God? I bowed my head and prayed for help, nearly jumping out of my skin when I felt a tap on my shoulder. "Liam!" The couple sitting three pews in front of me turned their heads and shushed me. I followed Liam outside.

Liam was a full foot taller than me. Today, he looked like he'd shrunk several inches. After giving me a bear hug he said, "I wasn't expecting to find you in the Chapel. Camille wanted a few minutes by herself with Father Joe, so I thought I'd say a prayer for Peg." He rubbed his unshaved face with his hands.

"Go ahead. I'll wait."

"Later. I'm anxious to hear what you've found out so far. Father Joe said we could use one of the empty classrooms. Let's go. I'll text Camille that you're here."

While Liam flicked on the fluorescent lights, I pulled a couple of chairs around one of the long tables. He pulled an envelope out of his sports coat pocket and slid it across the table, "I don't know what your usual fees are, but hopefully this will at least cover some of it."

"No way. I'm not taking it. This one is pro bono," I pushed the envelope back to him.

"I insist. Please take it."

I didn't want to argue with him, but I didn't pick up the envelope either. "Um ... I have a confession."

"If it's about the gun, I already know. That bungling cop, Sam, told me. Why did she have your gun?"

"Alex threatened her. She was upset. I'm so sorry. I loaned it to her until she could get one of her own. I never imagined this would happen." I struggled to keep my composure.

"He threatened her? Do you think Alex did it?" His jaw was set. I could tell he was angry.

"He has an alibi, but I'm not ruling him out."

Liam gazed at me sternly. "Liz, I know you thought you were doing the right thing loaning her your gun. This is not your fault. I want you focused on finding out who did it."

I stared squarely into his whiskey-colored eyes. "I won't let you down." I slipped the envelope into my purse. I could always donate the money to Peg's Foundation.

Camille entered the classroom seconds later. Her hazel eyes were puffy, and any remnants of mascara had been washed away. She crumpled into the chair on the other side of her husband.

"Oh, Liz."

"I'm so sorry, Camille."

"Please fill us in on what you have so far," Liam interjected, placing his palm on top of his wife's hand.

I shared my progress to date, leaving out that I had identified Chantal as a possible suspect. They already had enough to deal with. I felt awful I didn't have a more concrete report to give them. They deserved answers. And I sure wasn't bringing up some vague family secret. "May I ask you a few questions?"

"Please do," Camille said.

"Do either of you know of anyone who might have wanted Peg dead?"

Both of them shook their heads emphatically. Liam squeezed Camille's hand.

"How can the police be so sure it wasn't a break-in?" Camille asked. "Peg always carried a lot of cash. I hated that." She dabbed her eyes with a tissue with her free hand.

"Have either of you checked to see if anything is missing?"

"Not yet. The cops are releasing her place tomorrow. The clean-up crew will be there in the morning." Camille hesitated before continuing. "I need to pick up some items before the funeral. Liz, will you help me choose her outfit?"

"Of course." I was touched and terrified. Peg's outfit. The outfit she would wear to her grave. I dreaded it. Just the thought of it made my heart hurt. "Was there anything odd or unusual going on with Peg lately?"

Camille shook her head. "I just talked to her Wednesday. She was happy. We were planning a shopping trip for the following week."

Fishing for the family secret, I asked, "Anything I should know? Any problems in the family?"

Camille and Liam looked at each other. She gave him a small nod. "Jackson's in trouble for drugs again. He was arrested yesterday."

Jackson was their grandson and Jenny's younger brother. Their dad, Paddy, was Peg's oldest sibling. His wife had died of breast cancer when Jenny was in high school. They'd been married since their senior year of high school. The whole family had been devastated. Peg constantly worried about her brother, her niece, and her nephew.

"I'm so sorry. You both have so much to deal with. How's Paddy handling it, and what's going to happen to Jackson?"

I remembered that Peg had bailed him out of jail the first time. At sixteen, he was busted for using drugs. He didn't want to call his dad, so he'd called his aunt. He had troubles on and off ever since, but this time would be different. Jackson had just turned eighteen and was no longer a juvenile. A senior in high school, he was a smart kid set to graduate this spring. He was supposed to attend The Citadel in the fall but couldn't seem to get off the path of self-destruction.

"We don't know what will happen to Jackson. Paddy's torn up. He's trying to get him out of jail in time for the funeral." Liam glanced at the clock on the wall. "Camille and I truly appreciate all the work you're doing Liz."

"I'm sorry I don't have more to tell you. I promise I won't rest until I find out who killed Peg." My voice caught on her name. I stood to say my goodbyes, the emotions of the day engulfing me. Sobbing, I clung to Camille for a few minutes before relaxing my grip.

After parting ways, I stepped into the sanctuary, and lit a candle for both Peg and Jackson.

Chapter 8

As soon as I walked into the house, my cell phone started buzzing. It was Peg's friend from high school. "Hi Karen, how are you?"

"Not so good. I was wondering if you're free for a drink. I really need to talk about Peg. I just dropped Melanie off at Mom's, and Scott's Fantasy Football League has a meeting tonight, so I'm free after running a couple of errands. Can you meet at The Office around five?"

The Office was a nice bar South of Broad close to Rainbow Row, within walking distance from my house. People enjoyed telling their spouses and significant others that they were at The Office when in reality they were at a bar.

"Sounds perfect. I'll see you there."

After taking Duke on a nice long walk, I changed into my white jeans and a black-and-white striped long-sleeved cotton shirt, adding a pop of color with a hot pink necklace and earrings. I slipped on my black flat espadrilles and filled Duke's bowls with food and water. "Be home soon. Be a good boy."

I never tired of the walk down Rainbow Row. The historic Crayola-colored homes looked different depending on the light. The landscaping and window boxes changed with the seasons. Tonight, the camellias and azalea bushes were showing off their colors and the scent of jasmine and gardenia floated on the early evening air. Spanish moss hanging from oak trees danced in the breeze.

Inside the bar, Karen was seated in one of the booths designed to resemble a shortened office cubicle. The tables were conference tables complete with conference-room chairs. The bar was set up like one long workstation with several laptops patrons could use, along with places to plug in their own electronics.

"Liz, I'm so glad you could meet me on such short notice. I'm devastated about Peg."

"Me too." Even though I knew Karen needed to talk, I was overwrought from my earlier conversation with Peg's parents. I needed to regain control of the emotions warring inside of me. Instead of elaborating on the comment about Peg, I changed the subject. "How's that adorable daughter of yours?"

"Melanie's a doll, but she's also a handful."

"Pictures please." I slid into the opposite side of the booth.

Karen pulled out her phone and opened her photos just as the server appeared, ready to take our drink orders. The twenty-something girl was dressed in a black cotton T-shirt patterned as a suit and tie paired with black pants. Placing a big bowl of popcorn in the middle of the table, she promised to be right back with our drinks.

Karen slid her phone to me and I scrolled through a few pictures of her daughter. "She's adorable. I love the one of her with the teddy bear."

"Thanks." Karen took her phone back, and grabbed a handful of popcorn. "I just love their popcorn. Do you think they use real butter?"

"I don't know, but let's pretend it's the no-calorie kind."

"Ha. I still have to lose another eight pounds to get back to my pre-pregnancy weight."

"Are you kidding me? You look amazing. Your arms are so toned."

Karen was wearing a coral silk sleeveless top that showed off her tanned arms. Her thick brown hair was pulled back in a ponytail.

"Thanks, Liz. Carrying a kid around does wonders. I'm just glad these capris have an elastic waist."

The waitress set our drinks down. "Y'all want to order any food?"

"Do you have time for a bite?" I asked Karen.

"No, I have to get back and feed the crew."

"I may get something to go," I told our waitress. She didn't seem too happy that we weren't ordering food.

As soon as the waitress was out of earshot, Karen blurted out, "I can't believe Peg was murdered. What was it like that morning?"

I took a deep breath and closed my eyes reliving the horrific images. "It was awful. Our neighborhood was a sea of red lights. No one knew what was happening."

"Have you talked to her parents? I want to call them, but I have no idea what to say."

"I saw them today."

Karen's hands flew to her face. "Oh my gosh. How are they doing?"

"They both look like they've aged ten years overnight. Liam asked me to investigate."

"Will you do it?"

"You bet. I'd already started before he asked."

Karen grabbed another handful of popcorn and silently munched while she absorbed that information. "What about the cops? How does that work?'

"The cops are taking this too slow in my opinion."

"I have some information that I don't know what to do with, and I don't feel comfortable approaching the cops. They'll just dismiss me as another crazy female."

"I don't blame you. What is it?" I took a big sip of chardonnay. The cool buttery liquid soothed my throat and took the edge off my jumbled emotions.

"I've been having dreams the last two nights. Nightmares. I know it will sound crazy, but a part of me wonders if Peg is trying to communicate with me from the other side."

Grabbing another handful of popcorn, I waited for her to continue.

"In my dreams, Chantal shoots her in a drunken rage."

I could understand why she wouldn't want to share this with the cops. Sam would probably give her some terrible nickname like Krazy Karen. And honestly, it did sound a bit too woo-woo, but I wanted to hear her out.

Karen continued, "You know that Peg and Chantal didn't get along, but for a while there it was really bad."

"How bad?" I asked.

"Peg would be at Chantal's place and dump all the liquor. Chantal would get furious, yelling and screaming about how much she hated Peg. Chantal was never violent, but I saw some of the texts she sent Peg. They were vicious. When Peg finally figured out she couldn't control Chantal's drinking, their relationship improved … some." She hesitated before continuing. "Do you think it could be Chantal …?"

"I don't know. She's on my list of possible suspects, but I haven't had a chance to talk to her yet."

"That would be so awful for Camille and Liam." Karen grabbed tissues as tears rolled down her cheeks.

"Since you've known the sisters for so long, tell me about their relationship when they were younger."

"It was a little tough on the girls with both brothers constantly teasing and rough-housing. Peg took it in stride and usually joined in, but Chantal was super sensitive and a tattletale. They were close until our freshman year in high school."

"What happened then?" I asked.

"Oh. The usual. We were trying to be 'cool' kids. Chantal was still in middle school. We were kind of mean to her. It wasn't cool for freshmen to hang out with kids in middle school. She finally gave up. She found her own clique her sophomore year and hit her stride in college." Karen shook her head. "Then she became involved with a wild crowd and well, you know the rest. I wish I could help her. I know it weighed on Peg's heart."

"Thanks for sharing this with me."

"I want to help." Karen absentmindedly rubbed her cheek. "Who else is on your suspect list?"

I hesitated a moment, but she deserved to know, and she could give me some background on Alex. "Her ex is right at the top."

"Alex? Sure, he's a jerk, but murdering Peg?" She waved her hand in the air in dismissal. "I just don't see it. I mean we all grew up together. Alex has always been a selfish spoiled brat who thinks he walks on water. He'll bend the rules, but he's a stickler when it comes to not breaking the law. It drove me crazy when we all started driving. He was the worst backseat driver ever."

I decided not to tell her about Alex's latest threat. "Did you know she was dating a guy in Paris? Bjorn?"

"Yes. She said he was loads of fun and very ooh, la, la. He's older, maybe mid-forties. Divorced, two daughters. Peg cooed over his accent. I didn't get the impression it was serious or that they were exclusive."

I wasn't sure exactly what ooh, la, la meant since Peg never bothered to share any details with me. Was I the only one who didn't know they were dating? "She never told me about Bjorn. Do you know why?"

Karen fidgeted with her napkin. "She did ask me not to tell you. When I asked her why, she said she wasn't ready to tell you yet. I think she was afraid you might go snooping. Maybe she wanted to discover Bjorn's history on her own."

I was silent for a few minutes as I tried to recover from the jolt of fresh pain.

"I'm sorry, Liz. Are you OK?"

"I will be." I sighed and then charged ahead. "What can you tell me about Brad?"

Karen's eyes became wistful. "You know I had a huge crush on him in high school. Peg tried to get us together. Unfortunately for me, Brad seems to prefer blondes He still looks like a walking dream."

I felt encouraged by the blonde comment. The next question was irrelevant but the words escaped my mouth before I could stop them. "Did he have a girlfriend?"

"Yes. Teresa." She spat out her name in disgust. "You know Brad's story?"

"Some …" I wanted to hear what Karen might know beyond what I'd gathered.

"His little sister and only sibling died when she was ten and he was thirteen. A drowning accident. He and Teresa started dating the following year. I never did like her, but Brad adored her, and the relationship seemed to help him recover. He followed her to USC. She dumped him his sophomore year for some other guy." She shook her head. "And then, his parents passed away a year later. They were on Flight 93 on 9/11. He was devastated, dropped out of college. Later, he somehow pulled himself back together. I know Peg played a big part in that. And look at him now."

"What happened to Teresa?"

"She married and moved to Southern California after college. That's where she was originally from."

The waitress interrupted. "Another drink, ladies?"

Karen glanced at her phone. "Oh man, look at the time. I better go pick up Melanie."

"I got this, Karen."

"Oh no. I invited you." She dug in her oversized purse for her wallet.

I rapped my fingers on the table to get her attention. "You can get it next time. Plus, I want to place a to-go order."

"Thanks, Liz."

"No worries. Give your daughter and mom a hug from me."

***

My next-door neighbor, Gwen, hollered at me just as I was unlocking my front door.

"Liz, you received a delivery." She ducked back into her house and walked over with a beautiful assortment of pink peonies and cream-colored roses arranged in an unusual metallic vase. "Whoever sent you these has excellent taste," she said with a big grin.

I set the to-go bag on the ground and buried my nose in the heavenly scent of the peonies before taking the arrangement from her. "I have no idea who this could be from."

"Come on, I'm dying of curiosity. Open the card."

I pulled the note out, ignoring Duke's barks. "Hmm, it's from Brad."

I read the message in silence.

Sorry again about the other day.

Brad

"Oh, my heavens, that gorgeous friend of Peg's? You lucky girl."

"Please, Gwen. Don't make a big deal out of it. He wanted to apologize for becoming emotional over Peg's death. That's all. Thanks for bringing this over."

"OK, if you say so," Gwen replied, her voice full of doubt. "Looks more like 'I really like you' flowers to me, but what do I know." She gave me a wink. "Have a good night."

I texted Brad a quick thank you before sitting down to eat my order of chicken tenders with honey mustard. While I ate, I wondered about Karen's response to why Peg didn't tell me about Bjorn. Did one argument affect Peg's trust in me around her dating life? We had talked about other guys she'd gone out with since. Why was she afraid I'd snoop into Bjorn's background?

Chapter 9

The next morning, Cassie showed up on my doorstep dressed in her bathing suit and cover-up, a towel draped over one arm. She handed me a chicken casserole topped with cheese that looked delicious. Cassie was an amazing cook and baker. Through the years, she'd often dropped off delicious dishes and desserts to both Peg and me.

"C'mon Liz, it's time for water aerobics." She tucked a stray lock of black curls under her bathing cap.

Our community offered a water aerobics class three times a week during the warmer weather. I was typically the youngest participant, and while I loved the class, I just didn't feel up to it today.

"I can't. I need to work on this case."

"Lizzie, you also need to take care of yourself. Look at those circles under your eyes. Now be a good girl and go put your bathing suit on. I'll wait right here. The exercise and sun will do you good. And don't forget to put on sunscreen."

Cassie could be bossy and determined. Peg and I had nicknamed her Sassy Cassie. I knew from the look on her face that 'no' was not an option.

"OK, but I need to make a quick phone call. I'll meet you there."

After placing the casserole in the fridge, I called Peg's niece, Jenny, and asked if she had time to meet with me today. She was free mid-morning. Realizing I'd never been to the foundation's offices, I asked her for the address. As far as I knew, Peg didn't spend much time there either, maybe half a day a week. Although she had a passion for the causes she supported, she didn't have time for the operations side of it. She often commented on how lucky she was to have Jenny, her "fave" niece. Changing into my bathing suit, I pulled my hair back in a ponytail and proceeded to our community pool.

The sun was shining in a cloudless blue sky that matched the color of the pool. My favorite instructor was teaching and we worked out to the tunes of Abba. Cassie was right. I needed this. For a whole hour, my mind didn't spin around Peg's death. The sun, water, music, exercise, and laughter lifted my spirits.

As we were walking home, Cassie reminded me, "Don't forget this Sunday is game night. My house. Scrabble."

On the second Sunday of each month, the women in our community gathered for an evening of entertainment and camaraderie. We played different games, rotating houses. I'd hosted Pictionary last month. I didn't want to go, especially without Peg, but it would be an opportunity to gather more information around the investigation. "I'll be there."

Back home, I hopped into the shower and let the hot water ease the remaining tension in my body. After towel drying my hair, I quickly dressed, slipping into a coral and turquoise Lily Pulitzer sheath with matching turquoise sandals. I added a coral necklace and earrings, powdered my nose, and gave my lashes a light coating of mascara.

I was always starving after the water and sun, so I chopped some leftover ham and scrambled some eggs, throwing in the ham and some Swiss cheese. Duke loved it when I cooked.

After devouring my breakfast, I placed the dishes in the sink and let Duke out to do his business. I lured him back in with a treat. "Be a good boy. I'll be back soon."

***

Pulling up to the office park, I parked my convertible in the closest slot to Peg's Foundation, Suite 107. The exterior of the building was a deep red brick. Green awnings with white lettering proclaimed the name and number of each suite. Climbing up the four steps, I pulled on the handle of the glass door. Locked. I pressed the buzzer and waited. Jenny answered in seconds.

A small mahogany desk and a couple of cushy dark green and ivory striped club chairs were the main furnishings in the reception area. The walls were a soft yellow, the floors a dark wood. Framed prints of Charleston were expertly placed on the walls. A few end tables were stacked with old issues of *Architectural Digest* and *Southern Living*. Glass vases filled with fresh yellow roses completed the décor.

I followed Jenny down the short hall to the office on the left. There was a second office on the right and a granite countertop at the end of the hall with a coffee pot and a small refrigerator. Jenny motioned to the office on the right with the closed door, "That was Peg's office."

"Where's your receptionist?"

"We have a part-time girl. She comes in a couple of days a week. She's attending the Art Institute, studying interior design of course. She's only been working for us for a couple of months. Do you want a cup of coffee or a bottle of water?"

"I'm fine, thanks." Jenny was one of the few people who made me feel tall. She was about four foot ten. When she stood next to Peg, she'd made Peg seem like a giant. Today she had on white capris with a brown and white striped top and chocolate-brown espadrilles, which added another inch to her height. Silver hoops, a hammered silver necklace, and about twenty silver bangles completed the ensemble. No rings.

"Come in, have a seat." She motioned me into her office. She kicked off her shoes and sat in the chair behind her desk.

I took in the surroundings. Thank you letters and awards decorated the walls in her office. Tall black metal filing cabinets lined two of the walls. Jenny's desk was fairly organized. Behind her desk was a window with a view of the parking lot. Underneath the window, a credenza was piled high with stacks of paper anchored by two pots of fake ferns. Her cropped, copper-colored hair shone in the afternoon sunlight streaming through the open blinds.

Jenny pulled her legs up into the chair and hugged one of her knees. "What can I tell you about the foundation?"

"Everything." I settled into a chair in front of her desk.

"OK." She smiled. "It was set up as a charitable trust eight years ago, with a twenty-year life. For the first two years, Peg ran it herself with part-time help from various students from the Art Institute. That was back in the Alex days. I think she liked the escape. Whenever I was home from college, I'd help out. I love the mission of the foundation."

I held up a hand. "Remind me of the mission."

"To provide homes for the homeless. Including homeless pets. We talked about changing the name to match the mission. Now I'm glad we never did. During my senior year, Peg asked me if I'd consider running the foundation. That was a year after mom passed. The foundation was a lifesaver for me. I loved working with Aunt … Peg." Her voice caught on Peg's name.

Jenny briefly closed her eyes then reopened them. "My grandparents are devastated. Dad too." Grabbing a Kleenex, she tried to wipe away the tears running down her freckled cheeks. "I'm sorry. At least my mascara is waterproof." She managed a small smile.

"I heard that Jackson's in jail."

Jenny chewed on what was left of her nails. "Yeah. Dad's bailing him out."

"We can do this another day …"

"I'm OK, Liz. Let's keep going."

"Let me know anytime you want to take a break." I took a deep breath and continued. "Lately, how often did Peg come into the office?"

"When she was in town, she came in every Friday for half a day. We'd go over reports and catch up and then grab lunch."

"Did she seem any different these last few weeks?"

"No. Although I have to admit, lately the conversation was mostly about me. I'm dating a new guy and redecorating my condominium. I wanted Aunt Peg's advice." Closing her eyes, she pinched the bridge of her nose.

My heart ached for this young girl. "What happens to the trust now that Peg's gone?"

Jenny sighed. "It'll be around for another twelve years. Aunt Peg and I talked about it when I signed on. I'll continue to run it. After I heard the news, I thought about giving it all up. Maybe finding someone else to run it, but I changed my mind." Jenny sat up taller. "I have to carry on her work. I'm not going to let Aunt Peg and her legacy down."

"She was always so proud of you." I smiled remembering how fondly Peg spoke of her niece. "Did you guys go to lunch that Friday?"

"Yes. We went to Butcher and the Bee."

"That place is so good. What'd you guys talk about?"

"Work … and … I had a date with Lawson later. I asked her about … well … you know." She turned bright red and then confessed, "I spent the night at his house. It was our first time together. I couldn't wait to tell Aunt Peg how it went.'"

There was no way this adorable girl with a huge heart murdered Peg and I mentally crossed her off the list of suspects. Sometimes you had to go with your gut. "I know she would be so happy for you, Jenny." I sighed, to be young and in love. "Besides you, who else in the family was close to Peg?"

"Hmm, Aunt Jane. And of course, her brothers. I guess you know Chantal and Peg weren't close," she replied.

Aunt Jane was Peg's favorite aunt. "Who might know the most about the family's past history?"

Jenny frowned. "Probably Aunt Jane. Why do you ask?"

"Just something I need to follow up on."

"C'mon, Liz … spill."

"I'll tell you more later. Would it be OK if I spent some time going through Peg's files?"

"Of course. I have a key to her office. You're welcome to look through whatever you want. I haven't had the heart to even open the door."

"By the way. Have the police contacted you?"

She shook her head. "I keep expecting to hear from them."

Jenny unlocked Peg's office. "Here are the keys to the file cabinets. Let me know if you need anything."

"Thanks, Jen."

The interior of Peg's office had the pale yellow walls as the rest of the suite. A small mahogany table sat in one corner surrounded by four tufted chairs upholstered in a fabric covered with yellow roses. Peg's walls were decorated with original watercolors of dogs and cats from a local watercolor artist we both adored. The watercolors were framed in black making the artwork stand out against the pale walls. A bookcase lined the wall opposite the table. Along with a small collection of books, the bookcase contained awards and pictures from various events, including several pictures of Peg and me. A thin layer of dust covered the desk. I ran my finger along the desk, yearning to turn back the clock to those times.

Behind the desk was a credenza. I proceeded to unlock the cabinets and familiarize myself with Peg's filing system. The files were alphabetic and meticulously labeled. I started with the financials, pulling out the last quarterly report. Opening my notebook, I jotted down information. The foundation was healthy with cash. Operating expenses seemed reasonable. I made a list of all the charitable organizations the Foundation donated to last quarter and then proceeded to pull the file for each of them. There were only seven. Apparently, Peg preferred to make big contributions to fewer organizations. Miracle Haven, South Carolina Housing for the Homeless, Crisis Ministries, Carolina Lab Rescue, Charleston Animal Society, South Carolina Dog Rescue, and a fundraiser for Habitat for Humanity. The file for each organization contained a list of contacts, preferences, and donations/grants. Some of Peg's family sat on the board of Miracle Haven, Charleston Animal Society, and Crisis Ministries. I was not surprised. As I said, Peg came from old money. I reviewed the financials for any patterns to the donations or anyone who dropped off the list and might carry a grudge. One donor, in particular, jumped out at me: Peg's friend, Brad. I made a note to ask Jenny about his involvement in the foundation.

I pulled open the desk drawers. Inside the left-hand drawer was a yellow legal pad with a long, numbered to-do list, thank you notes to write, gifts to buy, RSVPs to make, etc. Two items caught my interest. Number twenty-one, contact Tina's parents, and number thirty, write Bruce a thank you note. Our neighbor, Bruce? Why did she need to write Bruce a thank you? I didn't see his name included on the list of donors.

A manila folder labeled "Tina" sat underneath the legal pad. Inside were handwritten notes with dates. *Spoke with Tina on 2/12 asked her to please consider visiting Miracle Haven. Told her I'd go with her.*

Miracle Haven was a homeless shelter for women. It particularly catered to women with mental illness.

2/2—It was freezing last night. No sign of Tina. Hope she had a warm place to stay.

3/1—Tina spent the night, slept on my couch; at least she took a shower. More dates and notes. *The last one 5/15—Brought Tina food and water, still camped out under the bridge.*

The file was about half an inch thick. Tina was a schizophrenic homeless woman who lived under the bridge a couple of blocks from us. Peg was determined to get her off the streets, and Tina occasionally stayed with Peg. Especially if it was freezing cold or blistering hot. Come to think of it, I hadn't seen Tina in a while. I tried to remember the last time. Before Peg's death—maybe a week or so? I wondered if she'd seen something that night that scared her off. I promised myself I'd search for her. Not only because she might be able to provide information, but also because Peg would want me to find her. I jotted down the contact number for Tina's parents. Realizing that I was just now noticing her absence, I flushed with shame. It was sad and true that the homeless could be invisible.

Jenny popped her head in. "Hey Liz, you're welcome to stay, but I've got to go. I have an appointment with one of our donors."

Placing the file back in place, I closed the drawer and glanced at my phone. It was past one. "I'm finished for now, but I may have some follow-up questions. When's a good time to contact you?"

She shuffled her foot and then softly said. "Um. If you don't mind …?" She swallowed hard and continued. "Will you go to lunch with me for the next couple of Fridays?"

My hands instinctively flew to my heart. "Oh, of course. I'd love to. Why don't I come around one o'clock this Friday? I have a couple of items I need to take care of in the morning."

"That works. Guess I'll see you tomorrow."

Tomorrow. Thursday. Right. Peg's funeral.

Jenny and I were getting ready to walk out when I spotted the patrol car. "Crap. Looks like the cops finally showed up."

"What do I do? I'm supposed to be at the donor's home in twenty minutes."

"You don't have to talk to them now. They can come back." I peered through the window. Sure enough, Sam and Matt were making their way to the door.

"I know these guys. The older one, Sam, is a pain and not very sharp. The other one, Matt is better. Let me handle it."

"Thank you," she mouthed as the buzzer sounded.

Sam and Matt introduced themselves, and Jenny motioned them in. Sam's cloudy brown eyes grew wide when he saw me. "What are you doing here?" he snarled.

"I was invited." I growled in response. Sam got in my face and shook his finger at me. "You better not be meddling. Or destroying evidence." His breath smelled like stale coffee.

Matt put his hand on Sam's shoulder. "Sam, c'mon."

He backed off slightly. His face was red. He pivoted to face Jenny. "I have some questions for you, young lady."

Jenny caught my eye and then found her voice. "Sir, I'm afraid we'll have to do this another time. I have an appointment in twenty minutes."

"Can't you reschedule?"

The silence hung heavy in the room and I could tell Jenny was torn. Matt spoke up. "Maybe it would be better if we came back later."

Sam considered the comment and then handed Jenny his card. "Fine. We'll be in touch." He pointed his finger at me and grunted. "You. Stay out of it." Grabbing Matt's arm, he marched out the front door.

***

I was due to meet Camille in half an hour. I dreaded helping her pick out Peg's outfit. I was contemplating what she would choose to wear when I received the text that Camille had arrived at Peg's place.

Camille greeted me at the door. Stepping inside, I noticed that the cleaning crew had erased all signs of the murder. Nothing looked out of order. Camille must have tidied up the place as well. I followed her into the bedroom.

"Would she want to wear something she might wear to church?"

Camille rubbed her arms, as if she was trying to comfort herself. I couldn't imagine the pain of picking out your daughter's burial outfit. I'd been turning ideas around all morning, and even though Peg's faith ran deep, a church outfit was not what she'd want to be buried in. I was sure of that. "How about something joyful. As if she was going to a welcome-home party?"

By the slight smile Camille gave me, I realized she'd caught my meaning. I hoped the thought of Peg being in heaven brought her mother some comfort.

We stepped into Peg's walk-in bedroom closet. There was plenty of room for the two of us. I reached for a flowing silk purple and white polka dot blouse. "What about this?"

Camille grabbed a pair of white chiffon wide-legged pants. "Purple was her favorite color. Wouldn't it look gorgeous with these?"

I walked over to Peg's shoe rack. There must have been two hundred pairs of shoes. Fortunately, they were organized by color and style. I picked up a pair of silver strappy Jimmy Choo sandals. Camille smiled and nodded.

"What about jewelry?" I asked.

Placing the items on the bed, Camille pulled a jewelry case out of her purse. Opening the case, she removed a double strand of pearls with matching earrings. "These were my mother's. I'd planned on giving them to Peg on her wedding day, but Alex gave her a diamond necklace and earrings that she chose to wear instead."

"They're beautiful. But what about—?"

"Chantal?" she interrupted. "I have other jewelry for her. These belong to Peg, the oldest daughter." She set the jewelry case on top of the clothes and reached for the worn leather bible embossed with Peg's initials sitting on the nightstand. Clutching it to her chest, she plopped down on the bed and started crying. "Her first communion."

I sat next to her and put my arm around her. "Why don't I give you a few minutes?"

Camille nodded.

Leaving Camille still sitting on the bed, I stepped out of the bedroom. This would be a good chance to take a look around. Maybe see if I could spot anything amiss.

Wandering through each room, I didn't discover anything missing. Even her secret stash of cash, buried underneath the sugar bag in a kitchen canister, was still there.

I mentally crossed off the possibility of Peg getting killed in the midst of a robbery gone bad.

Chapter 10

Sunlight filtered in through the stained-glass windows of St. Michael's Church, casting prisms of colored light onto the altar. Children too young to understand a funeral were squirming in their seats. Row upon row of black dresses, black hats, and black suits filled the sanctuary. I never knew so many shades of black existed. The who's who of Charleston were in attendance in all their glory. I was touched that so many members of Charleston's police force showed up in full dress. Their royal blue crests were the only relief in the sea of black. Programs with Peg's picture were being used as makeshift fans against the Charleston heat.

I sat twelve rows back behind the family. Our entire townhome community, minus Bruce filled the row. He couldn't get off work. The wooden pew felt hard against my thighs and back. The three-quarter-sleeve black lace dress I'd chosen to wear was a little warm. I remembered Peg's words when she insisted I buy it. "No girl can have too many LBDs. You have to buy it. It's perfect on you." At the time, I was imagining wearing my little black dress to galas and parties, not a funeral.

Lou and Cassie were sitting on either side of me. Cassie had on too much Chanel No. 5. I'd forever associate that scent with Peg's funeral.

The first eight pews were full of Kelleys. At the end of the front pew, Liam sat tall and stoic, his salt and pepper hair still thick despite his sixty-plus years. Camille was next to him, her petite shoulders shaking.

Peg's three siblings and their families filled the rest of the front pew. Peg's older brother, Paddy, sat next to Camille. The light from the stained glass windows reflected off his bald head. Jenny sat next to her father. Her brother, Jackson, was missing. I wondered if he was still in jail.

Ian, who was four years younger than Paddy and two years older than Peg, was next. Equal in height to Paddy, his auburn hair appeared to be freshly cut. His wife, Irene, was a head shorter, her blonde hair swept up in a bun. Their fourteen-year-old twin girls were nestled between them. Their strawberry blonde hair glistened in the light.

Peg's youngest sibling, Chantal, sat at the end, her auburn hair hidden under a wide-brimmed black crepe hat. There was no way to tell from this distance if she'd been drinking.

Aunts, uncles, and cousins filled out the remaining seven pews. Brad was sitting on the third pew next to Peg's Aunt Jane.

The Thomas family, Alex's family, took up the next three pews. I squirmed with disbelief that Alex had the nerve to show up.

Never before had I been so intimately involved with the individuals in an investigation. I hated that I couldn't see any faces. I wanted to know who was crying and who was not. A part of me grieved the loss of my best friend. Another part of me wanted to pull out my index cards and get to work.

The sound of the organ alerted us that the service was about to begin. We all stood as the priest headed down the aisle. Peg's casket followed, carried by other family members. Lou clutched my hand. I squeezed back trying to offer some comfort. Paddy, Ian, and Brad walked to the podium for their respective Bible readings. With Father Joe's eulogy, the floodgates opened. I was no longer Liz, private investigator. I was Liz, Peg's best friend.

The graveside ceremony took place at Magnolia Cemetery, north of the church, on the riverside. The ground was wet and soggy from last night's rains. The tent wasn't large enough for all the folding chairs neatly lined up in rows. At the front of the tent, metal buckets filled with white roses were available for anyone who wished to put a rose on Peg's grave. Several arrangements from the altar at the church surrounded her casket.

"Where were your parents?" I asked Lou as we walked into the tent.

"I told them not to come. They barely know the Kelleys. Other side of the railroad tracks," he replied. "I'm surprised your folks didn't drive up."

Lou and I shared a common bond of being only children. "They've called me practically every day." I sighed. "I convinced them not to come."

We found empty seats next to the twins. Ninth graders at the local Catholic school, they were at that awkward teenage stage. Everyone exchanged condolences and a few pleasantries as we waited for the ceremony to begin.

At best, only half the crowd that had filled the church was here, and I wondered if some folks went straight to the reception at the Kelleys' Kiawah home instead. I noticed Brad sitting next to Ian and Irene. He turned to look around and waved at Lou and me.

By the time the graveside ceremony was over, my mind and body were numb with grief. Lou and I stopped by the restroom before heading to the reception. Brad caught me as I was walking back to my car.

"Liz, I've been looking for you. I wanted to apologize again for the other day."

"No need. And thank you for the gorgeous flowers," I replied, noticing how handsome he appeared in his black suit and starched white shirt. I was touched he wore a purple tie, Peg's favorite color. "See you at the Kelleys."

"Wish I could. I hate to miss it, but I can't make the reception. I'm meeting some investors in New York. It's been set for weeks. Heading straight to the airport from here, but I'll be back late tomorrow."

"Safe travels."

I found Lou by my car having a smoke. We agreed to put the top down, and I tied a scarf around my hair to protect it from the wind. Lou started singing Aaron Neville's, "Don't Take Away My Heaven," as I fired up the engine.

"Please, no, Lou. It's too much," I pleaded. Plugging my phone in, I pulled up my jazz and blues playlist. The sound of the wind and the music were soothing as we set off on the long drive down the two-lane road. Oak trees dripping in moss arched over our heads. Lou and I were silent for most of the drive. I was relieved he didn't break into another random song.

Arriving at the Kelleys, I put the top up on my car. You never knew when a pop-up storm might happen. I refreshed my lipstick and fluffed out my hair.

"Hey Liz, I need another quick smoke," Lou said as he lit up a cigarette. "I'll meet you inside."

Climbing the steps to the Kelleys' home, I inhaled the smell of the ocean. My black stilettos were muddy from the gravesite. Peg would've loved that I wore them. I wiped them off the best as I could on the doormat and stepped inside.

The view of the Atlantic Ocean from the great room never failed to astound me. Floor-to-ceiling windows framed a caramel-colored beach and the ever-changing colors of the salt water. Today the ocean was shades of green, the sky a cornflower blue, with powder puff clouds tinged with gray. The rolling waves were rough, colliding on top of each other with sprays of white foam.

To my left, the great room opened into the dining room. A long table was laden with Southern comfort food. Shrimp, oysters, crab cakes, roast beef, green beans, carrots, sweet potatoes, mashed potatoes, cheese grits, various salads, pecan pie, strawberry shortcake, and cheesecake. The sight caused my stomach to grumble. Cobalt blue china rimmed in silver, linen napkins, and real silver were lined up along the buffet on the back wall. Vases full of white roses and purple hyacinths, Peg's favorites, had been placed in each room. I sighed. Her reception, just like Peg, was lovely.

As I searched the crowd for Liam and Camille, Peg's brother, Ian, came over and wrapped his arms around me in a big bear hug, careful not to spill his drink. His mustache tickled my face.

I squeezed him tight. "I'm so sorry." Stepping back, I noticed his auburn hair had thinned since I last saw him. He had circles under his hazel eyes.

"It's been rough. I'll feel better once the killer is behind bars." He took a gulp of his whiskey. "Dad said you're investigating. Do you have any leads?"

Ian was the second oldest in the clan of Kelley siblings. Peg adored him. I could hear the agony in his voice. "I don't know, Ian. I've just started."

"You were with her that night. What did she say?"

"She had words with Alex. She was upset."

"That bastard. I can't believe he even showed up for the service. The nerve. I'm glad he had the good sense not to come to the house. I know our families go way back. Still the way he treated Peg. It's just not right." His brow furrowed and he gripped his glass of whiskey tighter.

My thoughts, exactly.

"Did she finally tell him about Bjorn, the guy that she was dating?" Ian asked.

"Are you kidding? No. They argued about money. Alex had called asking for another loan, and she told him no."

Geez. Did everyone but me know about Bjorn?

"Well, it's about time." And then we both realized there would not be another time. Ian's shoulders slumped, and he excused himself.

Spotting Peg's parents, I headed their way. I embraced Liam and then Camille. She seemed reluctant to release me.

"Everything's lovely. Peg would have loved the flowers," I said.

Thank you." Camille's emerald eyes were rimmed with red, and a handkerchief was clutched in her right hand. Others wanting to offer their condolences came forward, so I stepped back to give them room. Liam grabbed my arm as I was walking by.

He leaned his head toward mine and softly said, "Please keep us posted. Call me anytime."

"Of course."

Making my way through the crowd, I found Lou standing by the drink station. He handed me a glass of sweetened iced tea with mint and lemon. Just what I needed to quench my thirst and soothe my insides.

As I sipped the tea, I scanned the room spotting Peg's friend, Karen, talking to a swaying Chantal. If Chantal hadn't been drinking before, she certainly was now. Karen's eyes caught mine with a silent plea for help. I pasted on a smile and walked over.

"Chantal, I'm so sorry about your sister." My shoulders tensed and my stomach clenched.

"Thanksss," she slurred. "We were just, uh, talking. What were we talking about? Oh. That time at the gala. Remember when Peg botched the mayorsss wife's name during her speech?"

I rolled my eyes at Karen. "That was pretty funny, Chantal. Do you remember how she recovered and had everyone laughing after that?"

"Well, that was Peg for ya. Alwaysss on the ball. I'll be right back." She teetered off spilling chardonnay in her wake.

Karen reached out and grabbed my hand. "Thanks for saving me."

"That girl's a mess." I couldn't imagine how uncomfortable Karen felt talking to Chantal after our conversation about her nightmares.

"I miss Peg so much." Karen attempted to wipe her tears away with a cocktail napkin.

I searched my purse for Kleenex as the tears rolled down both of our faces. Her husband, Scott, approached and handed her a drink. His presence seemed to settle her.

Spotting Ian's wife, I excused myself. "I need to give my condolences to Irene. Karen, call me anytime you need to talk. We'll get through this—somehow."

Irene's gray eyes, framed by long black lashes, misted when I greeted her. "I'm so sorry."

"Thank you. It's good to see you. I wish the circumstances were different."

"How are you guys holding up?" I asked.

"Like we're on a roller coaster. And there's still so much to do. I feel like I'm in a fog."

"I can't imagine. Please let me know what I can do to help."

"Thank you." She motioned toward the table. "I was just about to grab a plate. Camille put so much work into the menu. Please join me." She grabbed a plate for herself and handed one to me.

I placed a few slices of roast beef on my plate and reached for the horseradish sauce. Adding cold asparagus, a crab cake, and blanched carrots with an orange sauce, I looked at my plate. Not much room for a slice of that enticing pecan pie. I was amazed to discover that I was hungry.

Ian approached his wife. "I'm sorry, Liz. I need to borrow Irene." Turning toward her, he said, "Chantal's a mess and it's upsetting Mom. Will you help me convince my sister to sleep it off in the back?"

Irene shook her head in dismay, then set her plate on a nearby table. "Sorry, Liz."

"Don't worry. I understand."

Balancing my plate and glass of tea, I walked out to the back deck. An infinity pool bordered the deck and overlooked the ocean. Jenny and Aunt Jane were seated at one of the many tables set up for the occasion. Each table was covered a in white linen tablecloth anchored against the breeze with an arrangement of flowers. Careful not to spill, I headed to their table.

Aunt Jane stood and kissed each of my cheeks. Aunt Jane was Liam's older sister by ten years. Not only was she Peg's favorite aunt, but she had also been like a grandmother to her. And she always treated me as if I were her niece as well.

She was dressed in a lovely deep violet chiffon top and creased black pants with sensible black pumps. An amethyst and diamond necklace, bracelet, and earrings completed the look. Elegant was a word I always associated with Jane.

Jenny pulled out the chair next to her. "Have a seat."

"Damn it to hell, Liz. Peg was not supposed to die before me." Jane said in a raspy voice typical of a former smoker. "I'll have to redo my whole damn will."

"Aunt Jane!" Jenny said.

I loved that despite her elegant demeanor, Aunt Jane could be quite colorful and direct. She always named the elephant in the room that the rest of the crowd pretended didn't exist.

"Liam said you're investigating. Trying to find her killer. How's it going?" She fingered her necklace. "Must be tough. That on top of grieving like the rest of us."

"It's going. Peg knew so many people and didn't have many enemies." I paused to take a bite of roast beef and then asked, "Do you happen to know of anyone she had troubles with?"

"Besides Alex?" Aunt Jane scowled. "You know I never did like that jerk. Too smooth. Too charming. Thought he was God's gift to women. You have to watch out for those types. I told Peg when they were dating to think long and hard. But of course, she was head over heels in love. When they divorced, I had to bite my tongue hard not to say I told you so."

Jane had never been married. However, she had plenty of experience in the dating department. She always joked that she liked to play the field. She claimed that marriage was way too boring for her and would cramp her style. Her latest "friend" was ten years her junior. Peg jokingly called her Cougar Jane.

"Nobody in the family?"

"Well there's Jenny's brother, Jackson, he's had some trouble with drugs and the law," Jane replied. Jenny sucked in a quick breath, and then began chewing her nails.

Aunt Jane swatted Jenny's hands away from her mouth. "You and I are going to get a manicure soonest. You need some of those acrylic nails. Break that nasty habit." She inspected her own perfectly shaped pink fingernails and continued, "And Peg told me that once she caught Jackson in the act of trying to steal from her purse."

Jenny's face flushed and she dabbed at her forehead with a napkin.

Aunt Jane patted Jenny's arm. "I'm sorry, hon. It's the God-awful truth."

"Where is Jackson?" I asked.

Jenny tucked her hands underneath her legs. "He got in a fight after he was released from jail. He was pretty banged up, so Dad told him to stay home." We sat in silence for a moment before she continued shaking her head. "My poor grandparents."

I felt terrible for Camille and Liam.

Jane slapped the table. "And I'm so mad at Chantal I could spit whiskey. How dare she disgrace herself and cause a scene for her parents. As soon as she sobers up, she will get an earful from me."

I didn't doubt that Jane would follow through on that threat.

Lou walked out onto the deck and caught my eye, his slight nod telling me he was ready to leave. I said goodbye to Jenny and Jane. "I'll see you tomorrow Jenny."

I needed to go home, take a hot bath and have a good cry. Then, rest my feet and let Duke curl up next to me on the couch to warm the chill I had inside.

Chapter 11

The next morning I woke early, determined to make some progress on the case. Before starting, I needed to find Tina. My B&E into Alex's place would have to wait until after lunch.

Tina loved Duke, so I brought him along for the search. Duke seemed to have a sixth sense when it came to behaving around Tina. He was always gentle and careful not to startle her. Not his usual wiggly 'so glad to see you' self.

After twenty minutes of walking, drops of sweat formed at the base of my neck. Luckily, a slight breeze off the water, and a bit of cloud cover, eased the heat. Selfishly, I hoped she'd already heard the news of Peg's passing. I dreaded telling her.

I found no sign of Tina in her usual spot under the bridge and no empty water bottles or fast food bags. This particular bridge wasn't a popular hangout for the homeless, which was why Tina liked it. For the most part, she preferred solitude and didn't trust easily.

Duke and I walked to a nearby gas station on a street corner. I asked the clerk working the register if she knew Tina. She nodded and said that she regularly took Tina a bottle of water or a bite to eat, but she hadn't seen her in a week. I handed her my card. "Please call me if she shows up."

The clerk nodded in return.

When Duke and I arrived back home, I punched the number for Tina's parents into my cell phone. I tried rehearsing the conversation, but the words escaped me. I'd need to wing it. Maybe it would go to voice mail, and I'd be inspired with the perfect script later. Of course, Tina's mother picked up on the first ring.

"Hello?"

"Hello is this Mrs. Edwards?"

"Yes. Who is this?" I noticed the trepidation in her voice. And it had surprised me when she answered. Who did these days when you didn't recognize the number?

"My name is Liz. I'm a friend of Peg's. The woman who helped your daughter sometimes."

"Oh my. I heard about Peg in the news. She was always so nice to us and Tina. I'm so sorry about your friend."

"Thank you, Mrs. Edwards. I'm calling to ask if you've seen Tina lately? I tried to find her today to tell her about Peg."

"She wasn't under the bridge?"

Not wanting to worry her I replied, "I didn't see her, but I'm sure I just missed her." Duke yipped in the background.

"I haven't heard from her since before Peg died. Peg used to be a lifeline for me, filling me in when I hadn't heard from Tina in forever. You know my husband and I have tried so hard to get her in a home. Peg too, but ..." Mrs. Edwards' voice caught.

I waited while she recovered. "Can I come by and see you and your husband? Tina was such a big part of Peg's life."

"Sure. Tomorrow morning around ten?"

"That's great. Where do you live?" I wrote down the address.

"Thank you so much, Mrs. Edwards."

"Please call me Susie. We'll see you then."

I glanced at the clock on the microwave, just enough time to get ready for lunch with Jenny.

I met her at the foundation, and we walked to a small deli a few doors down the row of businesses.

"The food is really good here," Jenny said. "Their salads are fresh. The Caesar and Greek are my favorites. If you're in the mood for a sandwich, the chicken salad is excellent, and the bread is homemade."

I opted for the chicken salad with chips. Jenny ordered the Greek salad with a cup of the soup of the day, tomato basil. She chatted for a moment with the owner while I picked up silverware and our drinks and settled at a table in the corner. Only two other tables of the dozen or so scattered around the eating area were occupied, but then it was past the time for the regular lunch crowd.

Jenny carried a tray with our orders and placed the prettiest presentation of a chicken salad sandwich I've ever seen in front of me. The chips appeared to be homemade.

"Looks fantastic," I said.

"The food is great. Peg and I came here a lot, but the menu is limited, so we also went in town at least once a month. Last month we went to Fast & French."

"I love that place."

"Me too." After a bite of salad and a spoonful of soup, she continued. "Aunt Camille and Uncle Liam did a beautiful job with Peg's service. What'd you think?"

"Peg would have approved," I replied. We ate in silence for a few minutes.

"Do you think you're getting any closer to finding out who killed her?"

"Honestly Jen, I'm overwhelmed. Peg knew so many people. It's hard to narrow it down. The obvious suspects are easy, but the rest, well …" I shrugged.

"Can I help?"

I hesitated for a moment and took another bite of my sandwich, the chicken oozing out the corners and tumbling back onto my plate. "Well, actually you can. Apparently, Alex stumbled on some type of Kelley family secret while researching his genealogy."

"Is that why you were asking about the family history?"

I nodded. "I don't think it's connected, and I don't want to upset your grandparents. But I do need to follow up on it just in case. If you're willing, it would be easier for you to poke around than me. Maybe you could start with Aunt Jane?"

"Of course. When I was a kid, I always wanted to be Thelma on *Scooby-Doo*. I love doing research."

"Get out. You're too young for *Scooby-Doo*."

Jenny pointed her spoon at me, "Liz, you are never too young or too old for *Scooby-Doo*."

I laughed and then continued. "There's no pressure. If you don't feel comfortable, just tell me." I tasted a chip. "These are amazing." Placing some chips on a napkin, I passed them to Jenny so I wouldn't eat them all. "Tell me about the foundation's top donors."

"There's quite a bit of family on the list. The top five are Aunt Jane, Peg's parents, the O'Connors, Brad, and believe it or not, Alex's real estate firm."

"Hmm, what can you tell me about Brad?" I asked.

"They grew up together. Peg adored him and they usually talked on the phone for at least an hour every couple of weeks. They became even closer after his parents died. You heard the story, right?"

"Yeah." I scooped up a bite of fallen chicken salad with my fork.

"He was devastated. Dropped out of college. Peg spent Christmas break with him that year. Talked him out of joining the military and talked him into getting into therapy. Somehow, he pulled himself back together and was back in school in the fall. He ended up developing software the U.S. government uses to sift through social media sites and the dark web to catch terrorists before they strike. As well as software that protects individuals from identity theft. He's loaded and very generous to the foundation."

"Does he have any other family?"

Jenny shrugged. "An aunt and uncle on his mom's side. He's not close to them. I think it's too painful. Of course, Liam and Camille feel like he's part of the Kelleys, and he's good friends with Uncle Ian."

"Did Brad and Peg date?"

"I asked Peg about that once. She laughed saying it would be like dating your brother."

"Was he ever married?" I asked.

"No. As Peg would say—just married to the job. I don't know if I'll ever get used to talking about Peg in the past tense. Each time I do my heart squeezes."

"Me too, Jenny. You OK with a few more questions?" I felt awful for Jenny. The loss of her mother and now the loss of her favorite aunt.

"Sure, I want to help however I can."

"Were there any donors who suddenly dropped off the list or were upset with the foundation?"

"No. I can't think of anyone. We have a steady stream of loyal donors. Sometimes the amounts fluctuate based on what they can contribute. We make our financials readily available, so donors and potential donors can see how the funds are distributed and spent. No one's ever questioned us on that, or our choice of charities."

Jenny sat taller. Well, as tall as she could. She was obviously proud of the foundation's track record. "What about the charities? How do you vet them and how do you choose which ones to support?"

"Peg insisted we be the ones to select who we wanted to support so there's no application process. Ninety percent of our annual disbursements go to charities in South Carolina. She wanted to make a difference locally. Once we identify a potential charity, we do our research, including vetting some of their clients. If we decide to take the next step, we schedule a site visit, interview the management, and review financials. The last step is to meet with the board. If we take it that far, we typically announce during the meeting what level of support we'll provide. And then once a year we conduct an audit. The results determine whether or not we renew and at what level."

"Sounds rigorous," I said.

"It can be time-consuming. I don't know how I'll do it all without Peg's help."

"Hey, did the cops ever follow up after their visit the other day?"

"Yeah, the grumpy one called me later that afternoon. Asked me a couple of questions like where was I that night, and what my relationship with Peg was like. We didn't talk long. Said he might need me to come into the station later." She frowned.

"You, OK with that?"

"I guess. It's all so … unreal. I've never even been inside the station before." She took a few bites of salad and then asked, "Did you get the notice about the reading of the will at Uncle Ian's next week? You'll be there won't you?" She tipped the cup of soup and scooped up the last spoonful.

I nodded. "I can't imagine why I was invited, but I'll be there. What picture are you bringing?"

Irene had requested that we each bring our favorite picture of Peg to the reading.

"Of course, you're included," Jenny said. "Aunt Peg always thought of you as family. My favorite picture is from a trip Aunt Peg and I took to Paris together after my high school graduation."

I needed to go through my pictures and determine which one to bring. "I don't want to walk in by myself. Do you want to go together?" I asked.

"That'd be great. I love my dad, but I'd rather go with you. And who knows if Jackson will come."

After lunch, I popped into a gas station restroom and changed into a T-shirt, shorts, and tennis shoes. Pulling my hair into a short ponytail, I added a baseball cap and tucked as much of the blonde underneath as possible. Time to check out Alex's place.

I parked in a church parking lot several blocks from Alex's condo on Society Street. Fishing my phone, keys, lock picks, and large black sunglasses out of my purse, I threw my purse and clothes into the trunk and walked the three blocks to Alex's place.

The condos were in a renovated warehouse with an alley that ran behind them. I was taking my chances with a little B&E in broad daylight, but Alex would be at work. I hoped the same was true of most of the neighbors. Keeping a sharp eye out for any cops, I walked up and down the alley three times before I was satisfied the coast was clear. I had an escape route planned in case Alex had an alarm system. Tugging my picks out of my pocket, I set to work on the door. The lock clicked open and I turned the handle. I quickly released it and ducked behind a dumpster in the alley. I waited a full ten minutes. No sirens. No beeping. No alarm system.

I let out a breath and hurried inside, locking the door behind me. I started my search with the pile of mail on the hallway table. Several past due notices from the electric company and credit card companies. A newsletter from the country club. Lots of junk. It looked like the pile had been accumulating for a while. I opened the hallway closet. It was overflowing with sports equipment: golf clubs, a tennis racket, a few footballs, some free weights, and a basketball. I didn't find any guns.

I dashed up the stairs to the main living area that encompassed the kitchen and living room in one large space. The walls were exposed red brick and the oak floors looked like they'd been recently polished. The marble countertops were spotless, and the dishwasher softly hummed. I wondered if I'd just missed the house cleaner. I couldn't picture Alex mopping his own floors.

A fully stocked bar anchored one end of the living space. Built-in bookcases contained a big screen TV, sports memorabilia, and trophies. Moving on, I started the search in the bedroom.

Someone had made the king-sized bed. I opened the night-stand drawer. Inside was a framed picture of Alex and Peg on their wedding day. Underneath the photo was a black leather ledger-type notebook. The insides detailed his gambling wins and losses. In the back, he'd listed people he owed money to, including payment amounts and dates. Using my phone, I took a picture of the entry for the night of Peg's murder. I snapped three more pictures of the three-page debtor list. After replacing the book and closing the drawer, I moved on to the walk-in closet.

Digging through pockets of jackets and pants, I found only loose change, business cards, and a couple of cigars. I spotted a fishing tackle box on the shelf above the center clothes rack. Standing on tiptoes, I pulled the heavy box off the rack. The box contained three small handguns, a sheathed knife, and boxes of ammunition. I snapped another picture and placed the box back on the shelf.

I'd just finished checking out the bathroom when I heard footsteps coming up the stairs. My adrenaline kicked my heart rate into the stratosphere. I scanned the bedroom searching for a place to hide or some type of escape route. Slipping out the French doors onto the balcony, I squeezed into the space between the barbeque pit and the wall. Alex's voice carried easily through the thin glass panes.

"Yeah, yeah Dad. I promise. It's just temporary. I just need some funds to carry me through this week. I promise I'll pay you back."

I heard Alex open the closet door, and I lost the conversation for a few minutes. When I picked up the dialogue again, he was talking to someone else.

"Hey, Jim. I left work early. What time are you heading to Myrtle?"

A cardinal landed on the railing and started chirping. I huddled deeper into the space.

"Count me in. I just gotta drop by the parents to say hi. You need me to bring any booze for the ride?"

It felt like an eternity before I finally heard a door slam. I climbed down the fire escape stairs and darted out of the alley.

Chapter 12

My nerves were shot after the narrow escape at Alex's place. I looked forward to a long walk with Duke. I stopped by our community's mailboxes to pick up my mail and ran into Bruce. "Hi, neighbor. We missed you yesterday."

"I'm sorry I couldn't make it. How'd it go?"

"Lovely, but incredibly sad. A lot of people were there. Peg's poor parents." I shook my head remembering the strain on their faces.

Snapping back into PI mode, I continued, "I was about to take Duke for a walk. You want to get Buddy and come along?" Bruce's pug loved to walk with my dog and they were quite the pair, with Buddy running alongside, his short legs attempting to keep up the pace. Duke would be ecstatic to walk with one of his favorite pals.

"Sure. Meet you by the path in ten."

As I was attaching the lead to Duke's collar, my phone pinged with a text.

Hey beautiful. Can I take you to dinner tonight?

Brad was calling me beautiful? I quickly fingered a response.

>   I'm beat. Long day. How 'bout I cook for you to-morrow night?

>   A home-cooked meal? I'm in! What time?

>   Around six?

Can I bring anything?

Just your gorgeous *self I thought but didn't type.*

>   Nope just you :)

Placing the phone back in my pocket, I patted Duke on the head, and we headed out for our walk.

Buddy and Duke greeted each other with tails wagging before we turned down our usual path. Often we let the dogs off-leash, but there were too many people out walking today. The clouds had cleared. It had turned into a beautiful sunny day with a rare north wind, which brought both the humidity and temperature lower. Bruce was still in his scrubs. "How's the head?" he asked.

"Much better, thanks. I only notice the sore spot when I'm washing my hair." I touched the spot on my head. "How are you doing?"

Giving Buddy a little more lead, Bruce said, "I'm having night-mares. I keep replaying finding her over and over in my sleep."

"That's probably fairly common. Have you talked to anyone about it?"

"I've considered it. I could make an appointment with the therapist at the hospital. I may if it keeps up. The last thing I need to do is mess up a surgery."

Duke worked his nose on an azalea bush. Buddy enthusiastically joined him, and Bruce and I spent some time untangling their leashes.

Bruce continued, "I keep feeling like there's something I'm missing. Like some important detail that's at the tip of my brain … I just can't access it."

"Describe to me again what happened that morning."

Bruce relayed almost verbatim what he told me before.

"Have you heard any more from the cops?" I asked.

"Yeah. I'm worried about that too. They called me in the day before yesterday and asked more questions. Asked me not to leave the city."

"I wouldn't worry about it. They pretty much told me the same thing. You know they can't enforce it?"

"Yeah. But Liz, I'm the only Black person in our townhomes. Even worse, Black male."

"Oh, come on, Bruce," I said.

"I know you don't think that way, but I bet some of our neighbors do. I know the cops do."

I sighed. He was right. I attempted to reassure him. "Don't worry. I'll get to the bottom of this. I promised Peg's dad I would."

"I wish I took some comfort in that," Bruce said.

Puzzled by his comment, I changed the subject. "I stumbled on a recent list of Peg's to-dos. She'd jotted down a note to write you a thank you letter. Do you know what that's about?"

Bruce kicked a fallen branch off the path. He hesitated for several seconds before he said, "I didn't go to the funeral yesterday because I volunteer at the clinic at the Miracle Haven shelter. I thought it was a better way to honor her memory. She was always sending notes to me filled with stories of ways in which I was making a difference. I kept telling her she didn't need to."

I stopped in my tracks. Duke tugged on the leash. This was what kept Bruce so busy. "Why didn't you tell anyone?"

"I dunno. Just feels like I'd be bragging. I prefer to keep quiet about it. I asked Peg not to tell. Please don't broadcast it to the neighbors, Liz."

"All right. How long have you been doing this?"

Bruce shrugged, "A couple of years."

That was a long time to keep a secret. Seems Peg was pretty good at that.

***

Shortly after our walk, I heard a loud rap at my door. Barging in, Bruce said, "I remembered!"

"OK," I said, a bit startled.

Bruce sat on the couch. Duke planted a paw on his knee begging to be petted.

"Hi, Duke," Bruce scratched Duke's back. "Remember, I told you there was something at the tip of my memory. The television. It was on. It caught my attention because it was on that sappy channel my ex, Hope, used to watch. Hallway?"

"The Hallmark Channel?" I knew Peg loved to watch their shows.

"Yeah, that's it. I saw a bowl of half-eaten popcorn on the coffee table. A blanket and pillow were on the couch, like she'd settled in but got interrupted."

"Any evidence anyone else was there?"

Bruce searched his memory for a few minutes. "Not that I can think of. I'll let you know if I remember anything else. I need to run. I just wanted to let you know as soon as I could."

"Thanks, Bruce. Hot date?"

Bruce grinned for the first time since he entered the room. "As a matter of fact, yes."

"Walk the dogs tomorrow so I can hear all about it?" I asked.

"Not unless you want to get up at five."

"No thanks, I'll pass. Have fun," I replied.

I made a quick run to the grocery store to buy the ingredients for tomorrow night's dinner. As I was putting the groceries away,

Gunner called and asked me to meet him for a drink. I finished putting things up and then traded my shorts for jeans and my T-shirt for a coral-colored blouse covered with cream magnolia blooms. I added some dangly earrings, slipped on some sandals, and called for an Uber. I didn't feel up to fighting for a parking spot.

Walking into Moe's Irish Pub, North of Broad, I blinked several times to adjust my eyes to the dimness. The bar was a favorite hang-out for both PIs and cops, and I'd been here a number of times before. Gunner nursed a beer, sitting by himself at his usual corner of the long counter. The crowd was sparse, still a little early for the shift change at the station.

"Hey, Gunner, mind if I join you?" I teased.

He resembled a sixty-year-old Colombo except with reddish-gray hair and minus the trench coat. He and Colombo were about the same height with the same bushy eyebrows and bulbous nose.

"Sit, Liz." Gunner patted the barstool beside him and motioned the bartender our way. "House chardonnay?"

"You read my mind."

"How's my Lizzie holding up?"

I reached for the glass moist with condensation and took a sip. "I'm doing OK. I miss Peg like crazy."

Gunner waited a beat and then asked, "What's the latest on the case?"

"I'm making some progress." I slid the envelope with Alex and Lou's fingerprints over to Gunner. "Any chance you can get someone to run these for me?"

"You should share this information with the cops."

"I will. Just hang with me on this, OK?"

Gunner nodded and tucked the envelope into his iPad case.

"What are you working on?" I asked.

"I'm tied up with that high-profile socialite murder case."

"Oh yeah. The one where the wife was supposedly cheating

on the husband. And the husband cheated on the wife, but didn't want the expense of a divorce, so he killed her."

"It's messy alright. I was working with the wife before her murder documenting her husband's affair. She was ready to call it quits and wanted the big bucks."

"So did he do it?" I asked.

"If he did, he hired somebody. That's what I'm trying to get to the bottom of right now. I have a couple of leads. But enough of that. Tell me about Peg."

"I have a handful of suspects. All with motive. Some with alibis. Some not. I'm thinking it wasn't premeditated. Maybe a crime of passion."

Gunner turned and looked directly at me. "You have yourself on the list?"

"You been talking to Sam? Surely you're not serious." Gunner motioned to the bartender for another beer. "Liz, you have to think like the cops, and you have to protect yourself. I thought I taught you better. You need to be able to prove you didn't do it. Cuz the word on the street is you're a prime suspect. After all, it was your gun."

"But, I've no reason to kill her," I protested.

"You know that. And I know that. But the cops don't."

"You're right. Maybe I'm too close to this case." I took a sip of my wine. "I sure don't like Sam. He has it out for me."

"Cut him some slack. He's an OK cop. Just a little crusty. Being on the force for a while can do that to you."

Rubbing my damp hands on my jeans, I took a deep breath and said to myself 'maybe.' I took another sip of wine and asked, "So, what else are you hearing on the streets? Any other suspects besides me?"

"Maybe Alex or that business partner of hers, Lou."

"Both are on my list, plus Peg's sister, Chantal. I did a little B&E into Alex's place today," I said.

"That's my girl. What'd you find?"

I recapped my findings and showed Gunner the pictures on my cell phone. I left out the fact that I nearly got busted. "What am I missing?"

Gunner thought for a moment, "Any of Peg's neighbors have security cameras?"

"Already checked. Nope. There are two cameras at the front entrance of our neighborhood. They haven't worked for months. Can I ask a couple of favors?"

"You know I'd do whatever I can for you."

"Will you ask the cops if any of the local businesses caught anything on camera? It'll save me a bunch of time."

"You got it."

"You have any connections in Illinois?" I asked.

"A few, why?"

"Bruce moved here from Illinois. I discovered he was temporarily suspended while he was practicing there. Even though it's a stretch that he killed Peg, I'd still like to know why he was suspended."

"I'll see what I can find out. Good work, Liz."

"One more favor? While you're working on your case, can you find out if any of these 'for hire' folks could have also killed Peg? I know it's a long shot they'd use someone else's gun, but I need to rule out the possibility that Alex hired someone."

He jotted notes on a napkin and stuffed it in his wallet. "I'm on it."

The front door opened wide and about a dozen cops headed our way, including Sam. Gunner and I changed the subject to the basketball game as Sam marched over.

"Gunner. Liz." He nodded to both of us before ordering a Guinness. "She better not be here to pick your brain about that decorator's case," he said, as if I wasn't sitting right there.

That man sure knew how to set me off. I started to stand up. Gunner grabbed my arm, gently urging me to sit back down.

"Nah, Sam. You know we're old friends. Just catching up. And by the way, that decorator's name was Peg and she was Liz's best friend."

"Sorry. Didn't mean no disrespect." Sam grunted as he took his Guinness and joined a group of cops at the other end of the bar.

"Thanks. I better go." I called for my Uber.

Gunner patted my arm. "Don't let Sam chase you off."

"No. Honestly, I have a thousand things to do. Call me when you find something out."

"You got it."

Returning home, I prepped the King Ranch casserole in anticipation of Brad's visit tomorrow. The prep work calmed me after the interaction with Sam.

After placing the casserole in the fridge, I sat at the kitchen table and added notes from my visit with Gunner. He was right; I needed more information on Lou. He was a neighbor, and he had a key to her house. He stood to gain the other half of the business. He had no verifiable alibi for the night, just at home asleep. And he had the capacity for violence. Maybe I could poke around his place. I had a key so technically it wouldn't be breaking and entering. Seemed like a lousy way to treat a friend, but I needed answers. I had already poked around the business and had come up empty except something niggled at the back of my mind.

Suddenly I realized what I'd missed. Why wasn't Peg's will in the locked filing cabinet? I found all her other important personal documents. Had Lou removed it before my arrival? He seemed to over-emphasize never touching the filing. A B&E into Lou's place loomed on the horizon.

Chapter 13

The next morning, I popped by Southern Charm on my way to the Edwards'. Ellie greeted me at the door of the shop and walked me back to my favorite table outside.

"Tea or coffee today?" She asked.

"Hot tea, please. And I'll take the quiche special."

Ellie returned with a tray filled with a pot of steaming tea, milk, and a prosciutto and shallot quiche with a side of fried green tomatoes that smelled amazing.

"Mind if I join you? My niece is watching the front, so I can take a break." Ellie sat across from me and filled two mugs with tea.

"I'd love the company."

"No Duke today?" Ellie asked as she poured milk into her tea.

"No, I'm headed to visit with Tina's parents."

"Who's Tina?"

"She's the homeless girl Peg had befriended. No one's seen her since Peg's murder, and her parents are worried about her." After stirring a packet of sugar into my tea, I took a bite of the quiche. The thin and flaky crust melted in my mouth.

"Oh my. You don't think something happened to Tina do you?" She blew on her tea before taking a sip.

"No. It's not unusual for us not to see her for a while. I just didn't want her to find out about Peg from someone else. They were close, and Tina will be upset." What if something happened to her that night? I pushed that thought to the back of my mind and prayed for her safety.

"How's the investigation? And how are you doing?" she emphasized the last words.

"I'm OK. And the investigations going slower than I'd like." I cut into a fried green tomato, a southern delicacy. I could taste the buttermilk in the batter. The tomatoes were perfectly fried. "Another winner, Ellie. You should permanently add these to the menu."

"Thank you." Ellie beamed and then frowned. "Do you have any idea who did it? I can't imagine anyone wanting to hurt sweet Peg. She was such an incredible person and so generous to the Charleston community. She leaves a big void."

After licking the fried bits of tomato off my lips, I replied, "I have a list of suspects. You know money can be both a blessing and a curse."

"What do you mean?"

"Money is one of the top motives for murder."

She gasped. "You think someone killed her for her money? Who?"

"A few people stood to gain from her death." I leaned forward to tell her more, but Ellie's niece interrupted us. "I hate to bother you, Aunt Ellie. It's getting kinda busy. I sure could use some help."

She turned toward her niece who was tapping her foot. "I guess we'll have to continue this conversation later. Take care of yourself, Liz." She patted my hand and followed her niece back inside.

***

I drove to the Edwards' home in Goose Creek, about twenty minutes from downtown Charleston without traffic. I easily located the 1960s red brick ranch-style home. Wiping my shoes on the welcome mat, I rang the doorbell.

Susie answered and invited me in. "Please, have a seat."

Her white cotton capped sleeve shirt showed off arms that had not seen the inside of a gym in a while. Her salt and pepper gray hair fell to her shoulders in a soft wave. Her chocolate brown eyes were etched with wrinkles. She looked sixty, but I guessed she was probably younger. Tina was in her mid-twenties. Susie smoothed the front of her khaki-colored polyester pants with the palms of her hands. "Can I get you a drink?"

I sat on the brown tweed couch in the living room. A rust, sage, and brown braided area rug tied in with the western artwork. "Some water would be great."

She left for a moment returning with a glass of water. I took a sip and then asked, "Do you have any other kids besides Tina, Susie?"

"No, John and I married in our mid-thirties. We were lucky to have Tina. You know she wasn't always this way. What do you know about schizophrenia?"

"Not a lot," I admitted.

"I didn't know much either until a doctor diagnosed Tina. That's when I became involved with NAMI."

"What's that?"

"The National Alliance for the Mentally Ill. At first, I spent a lot of time in denial, and we saw every doctor we could afford, hoping for a different diagnosis. Schizophrenia is a terrible illness. NAMI's been a life-saving source of education and support."

Pausing, she shook her head and then continued, "Tina led a normal life until she turned twenty. She made straight A's. Loved to play volleyball." Susie wiped a tear from the corner of her eye. "She was a junior in college when her whole demeanor changed. She became paranoid and dropped out. I never imagined our daughter would be living on the streets."

I could hear the anguish in her voice. "Peg told me how hard you tried."

"Peg was helping us get legal guardianship so we can get Tina into a place that can help her. We're set to go in front of the judge in three weeks. Technically, she's an adult so without that there's not a lot we can do. I hope we can find Tina before then."

"I'm sure you will," I tried to reassure her as a tall man walked into the room, bringing the fresh scent of Irish Spring with him. John bent down and kissed Susie's cheek.

"John this is Liz, Peg's friend."

"Hi." John offered his hand, and I shook it. Dressed in a suit and tie, he stood a couple of inches over six feet. I'm not good at guessing weight, but let's just say he hadn't seen the inside of the gym in a while either. His belly pouched over his leather belt. He eased his way into the worn leather recliner close to the sofa.

"I'm real sorry about Peg, she was good to Tina."

"Thanks. I know she cared a lot about your daughter.

John nodded, then said, "I'm about to head to work. But I have a few minutes. I'm glad you dropped by."

"Where do you work?" I couldn't think of too many places where someone would go to work in a suit and tie on a Saturday.

"I'm at Marcus Miller Cadillac off of Highway 26. Been there ten years." John leaned forward, adjusting his tie. "So … How can we help?"

"When did you guys last see Tina?" I asked.

John said, "About a week and a half before Peg died. Occasionally, Tina would ride the bus to have dinner with us, sometimes spend the night. She didn't stay that day."

"You haven't seen her since?"

John shook his head, and Susie chimed in. "We could go as long as a month without seeing her. We've been trying hard to find her." She turned toward her husband. "Johnnie, we need to find her before that hearing." Susie wrung her hands together.

I felt so bad for this sweet couple. "Will you make a list of all the places she likes and anyone who knows her? I'll try to find her for you."

Susie fetched her address book and a pad of paper. She and John spent a few minutes jotting down everything they could think of before tearing off the page and handing it to me. We exchanged email addresses and mobile numbers.

"I'll find her. I promise." I hugged Susie and then John before I let myself out the front door.

Once in my car, I reviewed the list: three shelters, a church, and several parks and bridges close to my house. The Edwards had also listed seven people who knew Tina. None of these people had phone numbers or addresses. Just names and brief descriptions of what they looked like, apparently all homeless like their daughter. I had a long day ahead of me.

After four tiring hours of searching, I went home depressed and longing to jump in the shower. Visits to three shelters and conversations with most of the individuals on Susie and John's list were not only fruitless but left me overwhelmingly sad.

Jo, the easiest one to talk to, seemed mentally healthy. After she lost her home in Hurricane Hugo, she found she loved the freedom of living on the streets. Her pit bull, Jack, and the knife she kept close helped her to feel safe.

Ed was in worse shape than Tina, and his hygiene left a lot to be desired. He emitted the smell of body odor and alcohol. Most of the other people I talked to were in similar straits as Ed.

Then there was Kipper. I spoke with him over a free lunch of meatloaf, green beans, and mashed potatoes at the second shelter I visited. Kipper had lost his job at Cooper Motors manufacturing plant when they downsized. When he couldn't make rent, the apartment management evicted him. He was trying to get back on his feet, but nothing seemed to be going his way, and he had no family.

Not one of them had seen Tina in the last couple of weeks. Nor did they think much about the fact that they hadn't. Apparently, it's not unusual for someone on the streets to suddenly drop off the grid. No one had any further suggestions about where she might be. I sent a quick text to Susie reporting the results. I promised that I wouldn't give up.

After a long hot shower, I felt restless and unsettled. I needed to burn off some steam. Changing into my workout clothes, I headed for our gym. When I walked in, I noticed that Maria and Linda were there working out. I said hello and hopped on a stationary bike next to Maria.

"How is the investigation going?" Maria asked.

"Slow. How was your week?" I punched in my weight, set the time for thirty minutes, and selected the mountain trail, level three.

"I had a coffee with Bruce. He's nice." Maria wiped the sweat from her neck with her hand.

"That's great," I responded.

"Taking it slow as you suggested. I kinda like him."

"Slow is good."

Maria smiled. "Will you be at Cassie's on Sunday?"

"Game night. Wouldn't miss it. Not that Cassie would let me if I wanted to." I laughed.

"Isn't that the truth? See you tomorrow, Liz." Maria climbed off the bike and waved goodbye to Linda.

Linda walked over, mopping the sweat off her face with a towel.

"Where's Tony?" I asked.

"Golfing."

"You didn't go with him?"

"No, Love. Too much to do around the house." She hesitated,

scanning the room. "Listen, I'm sure it's nothing, but I probably should have mentioned it earlier …" Linda let the words trail off.

I waited for her to continue while I pedaled, sweat dripping down my face.

"The week before Peg's murder, I was watering the plants out front. Cassie was at her bridge game. It was a school holiday and Gwen was home. Everyone else was out. Tony was golfing. Again." She rolled her eyes.

"OK," I said, anxious to hear the whole story.

"I saw Peg pull into her garage. I wondered why she was home mid-day. Not five minutes later Gwen was marching across to Peg's, a woman on a mission. She didn't even wave to me." Linda put her hands on her hips.

"That's rude," I said.

She nodded continuing, "Peg answered the door, and they had what seemed like a heated conversation, although I couldn't hear a thing." Linda pointed to her bad ear. "Didn't last long. Probably nothing. I just thought you should know, Love."

Hmm…maybe I needed to add Gwen to the suspect list. "Any idea what it could have been about?"

"No clue. You know Gwen. She can be sensitive. She needs thicker skin."

I nodded then asked, "See you tomorrow?"

"Wouldn't miss it."

Back home, I glanced at the time on my phone. Crap. Brad would be here in less than an hour.

After taking a quick shower, I agonized over what to wear. Flirty or the casual 'I don't care' look? I changed outfits three times before finally settling on a lilac lace V-neck short-sleeved shirt and a pair of faded fringed denim capris. I fluffed out my freshly dried hair with dry shampoo to give it some volume and texture. I slipped on my favorite Tom's khaki espadrilles and spritzed my neck with Philosophy's Amazing Grace perfume.

Checking my appearance in the mirror, I added a little eyeliner, another coat of mascara, and some extra blush.

I hurried downstairs, threw together a salad, and placed the King Ranch casserole in the oven. The doorbell rang just as I was wiping off the counters.

Chapter 14

Brad arrived at six, his arms full of goodies. "Hey, Duke. I brought you a treat." He reached into a paper bag and pulled out a huge rawhide. "OK if I give this to him?"

"Sure. He'll love it." I laughed as Duke took the rawhide and rolled around on the carpet in sheer delight. "I thought I told you not to bring anything."

"A gentleman never comes empty-handed." Reaching into another sack, Brad pulled out bottles of red and white wine. "I wasn't sure what you liked, so I brought both."

"Thanks. I'll put these in the kitchen. What can I get you to drink?"

"Scotch," he replied.

"Got it. Ice and a splash of water?"

"Great memory."

As I poured his scotch and my wine, I took a moment to compose myself. Brad's forest green short-sleeved polo shirt complimented his tan and showed off his biceps. His well-worn blue jeans were frayed where the threads met his ostrich cowboy boots. When he bent over to pet Duke, I couldn't help but notice how nicely his jeans fit his toned tush. Peg must be up there laughing at my barely contained lust.

Setting his drink on a coaster on the coffee table next to a bowl of mixed nuts, I placed my generously poured glass of malbec on the end table and folded into the blue and gray striped wing chair, a comfortable distance from Brad.

He looked me up and down with his gorgeous aquamarine eyes. "You look great."

Squirming in my chair, I managed to reply, "Thanks."

Brad grabbed a handful of nuts. "What was the reception like?"

"It was lovely and sad. Camille thought of every detail." My heart twisted at the memory of her grief stricken face. Swirling the wine in my glass, I continued. "How'd your trip go?"

"Productive, but I wish I could've stayed here instead. How are you holding up?" Sympathy emanated from his eyes.

I lost myself in those eyes for a moment.

"Liz? You OK?"

I sat up a little straighter and nodded. "Hanging in there. Some days it hits me hard, and I feel like I'm trying to wade through thick mud. Other days I try to tuck it away, so I can make progress on the case."

"You working any other cases?"

"A small one. Honestly, this is all I can handle and barely."

"Come here." He patted the space on the sofa next to him. "Not you, Duke." Brad gently pushed Duke's paws off the sofa.

I raised my eyebrows in question.

"Just trust me."

I moved over and he slid down to the end of the couch. "Now put your feet up."

Blindly, I obeyed.

Brad slipped my shoes off and slowly started massaging my feet. I couldn't help but let out a small "Oh."

"See. I'm a man of many talents."

"Mmmm," I could feel the tension melting, while butterflies fluttered to a fast song in my tummy. Placing my head on the sidearm of the couch, I closed my eyes. After several minutes of silent bliss, I said, "If you keep doing that, I'll fall asleep and the delicious casserole I have in the oven will burn."

Playfully tickling my feet, he said, "Ah, well, we can't have that."

"Quit that." I giggled, pulling my feet away. As I rubbed my toes, I became uncomfortable with the sudden intimacy and scurried back to the safety of my chair. "Thanks, I had no idea my body was so tense. That felt amazing. If you ever decide you want to quit being a CEO—"

"Ha. Fat chance." Brad interrupted. "And you're welcome. Listen, I know you need to do your thing and ask your PI questions so let's get that out of the way. Then we can just enjoy a night of each other's company."

I took a big gulp of wine. "Sure … um … I know you're a big donor to the foundation. I saw the records."

"Yeah." He picked at his jeans and took a long sip of scotch. "I always admired Peg's mission. It felt good to contribute to that, versus spending all my money on man toys." Placing the tumbler back on the table, he shook his head. "She was so vivacious. I thought she would way outlive me."

"Me too." I took another swallow of my wine, then glanced at him. "This may be way too personal, but, well, were you guys ever romantically involved?"

Brad gave me a big sheepish dimple-framed grin. "Nah. Everyone tried to make us an item. Drove Alex crazy in high school, especially the year she was Prom Queen, and I was voted Prom King. It was too weird. I mean, we used to take baths together when we were toddlers. We're like brother and sister. We couldn't make it happen. We were never attracted to each other in any romantic way."

Just then, the buzzer for the oven timer went off. Grateful for the interruption, I said, "Dinner. I hope you're hungry."

"Whatcha cooking?"

"King Ranch Chicken," I replied.

"Smells fantastic." He picked up his drink and the bowl of nuts and followed me into the kitchen. Duke led the way recognizing the buzz of the timer as having something to do with food.

Entering the kitchen, I called out. "Hey Alexa, play the Big Chill soundtrack." Turning to Brad I said, "I hope this music is OK."

"Are you kidding? I love the movie and the music. It's a classic. I saw it on a plane about five years ago."

I turned the oven off and pulled the salad out of the refrigerator. With the wooden salad bowl in my arms, I backed right into him, nearly dropping the bowl.

Brad reached his arms around me, steadying me, and saving the salad.

"Whoops. Thanks."

He pulled one hand off the bowl, brushed my hair to the side, and nuzzled my neck. "Mmmm, you smell good. What is that perfume? Peg used to wear it too."

"Amazing Grace," I replied.

"Well hell yeah and hallelujah. No, really?" He planted a tender kiss right behind my left ear.

"That's the name of the perfume, silly." I was amazed I could get the words out of my mouth. My whole body tingled, and I almost dropped the salad again. The doorbell rang sending Duke into a barking frenzy. Grateful for the interruption, I handed Brad the bowl and went to answer the door.

"Hi, Lou." Dressed in a short-sleeved starched white shirt, black pencil jeans, and black loafers, he looked like he'd just gotten off work. "Working on the weekend?"

"Yeah. I'm still catching up. The mailman put some of your mail in my box." He handed me a small stack of envelopes, and then looked beyond me. "I didn't realize you had company. Hi Brad."

Brad walked over and embraced Lou. "Good to see you, man."

"Good to see you too. You look great." Lou stood back and gazed at Brad.

Lou's once-over of Brad confirmed my suspicion that he had a slight crush on him. "Do you want to stay for dinner? I cooked King Ranch Chicken. There's plenty." Maybe I could quiz Lou about his schedule next week and find a time when I could check his place out.

"If I'm not intruding? I am starving." Lou said.

"No, c'mon we were just about to eat. I'll set another place."

Lou tried to make small talk with Brad as I set plates laden with King Ranch Chicken in front of each of them. Brad's frown and clipped response to Lou's chatter made me wonder if he was not happy with the extra company.

After a forkful of food, Brad's mood brightened a bit. "Mmmm. This is delicious."

"Thanks. I made an extra dish for you to take to Irene." I hesitated, then continued, "Next week's will reading will be strange. I'm kind of surprised that Ian is the executor. I just assumed it would be the oldest, Paddy."

"Ian oversees the family trust, so it makes total sense to me." Brad shoveled another forkful of casserole into his mouth.

"How's business going, Lou?" I asked, hoping to gain some information about his week.

"OK. I'm heading to Columbia to follow up on a project day after tomorrow. Not looking forward to the drive."

"Hope you don't have to be there too early." I topped off his wine glass.

"My appointment is later in the morning. Should be able to avoid most of the traffic."

Score. Immediately feeling guilty for the thought.

Alexa started playing, "I Heard It Through the Grapevine."

"Is this the Big Chill soundtrack?" Lou asked.

Mouth full, I nodded.

A far-away look formed in his eyes as he reminisced. "Peg and I watched this together a couple of years ago. A cold, damp day. The kind where you just want to hunker down and stay inside. You were in Florida visiting your parents. Peg asked if I wanted to come over and watch a movie. She popped a huge batch of buttered popcorn and fixed hot chocolate. We danced to this song and a couple of others. God, I miss her."

Once the song finished Brad said, "Hey Alexa, play 'If I Could Turn Back Time.'"

"Get out," Lou exclaimed. "You like Cher?"

"Of course. Don't you remember? Peg and I went to Vegas for our 30th birthdays. We left right after her big shindig at Irene's. We had front row seats for the concert. It was a crazy crowd. The best part was the people watching."

"I forgot you guys went to see Cher. I remember now," Lou said. "I was so envious." When the song ended, he said, "Hey Alexa, play 'If I Were a Rich Man.'"

Lou sang along, his deep baritone voice breaking up after the fourth stanza. "Sorry," he said wiping away tears with his napkin. "I remember the year I joined the Charleston Way Theater. Peg came to opening night. She was in the front row, beaming with joy as she watched me perform that song."

We ate in silence for a few minutes, then I couldn't stand it. "Hey Alexa, play Adele," I said.

Alexa selected "Hello." Lou and I caught each other's eyes and started laughing. Lou slapped his knee, "Oh my god, I remember when she sang this at karaoke night at the pub."

I stood up and did my best impression of Peg singing a horrid version of the song. I worked the improvised stage of my kitchen floor, playing to the audience and dancing to the beat.

"That girl never could sing," Brad blurted out in between guffaws of laughter.

Clutching his mid-section, Lou said between laughs, "Stop girl. You're making my stomach hurt."

The next song began, Lady Gaga's "Edge of Glory." Again, Lou and I looked at each other. It was like Peg was picking the songs. "Do you remember when the three of us went to New York City to see Lady Gaga?" Lou asked.

"That was such a blast. Peg booked a suite at the Waldorf for the weekend," I explained to Brad. "We had the best pajama parties."

"Oh, my gawd. Remember Saks after lunch and a few glasses of wine?" Lou continued grabbing my arm. "Taking selfies with the mannequins?"

My eyes misted over with the memory.

And just like that we were asking Alexa to play various songs and laughing, crying, singing, and dancing. Sharing Peg stories. By the time we finished, it was midnight and we were all tipsy. I was glad Brad was Ubering to Ian's, and Lou just had to stumble across the way.

"I had a great time." Lou kissed my cheek and then turned and embraced Brad. "I'll see you next week, Buddy."

Brad and I washed the dishes while he waited for his Uber. A honk announced the arrival of his ride. I pulled the other casserole out of the freezer, placed it in a paper bag, and walked him to the door.

"Thanks, Liz. Tonight was terrific. I'll see you soon."

Before I realized his intentions, he cupped my face with both hands and kissed me slowly and tenderly on the lips before gently exploring my mouth with his tongue. My body felt like it was on fire, yet, I felt a deep sense of peace flow through me. The second Uber honk interrupted us. I handed Brad the casserole and opened the door with one hand while the other clutched Duke's collar.

"Bye, Duke. Bye, Liz. Thanks again."

Exhausted, I just wanted to crawl onto the couch and go to sleep. The rest of the dirty dishes would have to wait. I managed to stumble to the bedroom and slip out of my clothes, letting them fall to the floor. Plopping on top of the bedspread, I shut my eyes. I had a hard time falling asleep because my mind kept replaying that kiss.

Chapter 15

Duke's incessant barking woke me out of a deep dreamless sleep. "What now, boy?"

Of course, it was only the neighborhood tabby licking her paws right in front of our door. I gave him my usual lecture about ignoring the cat, which made absolutely no difference to the steady stream of woofs until I mentioned the word treat. Duke left his post and followed me into the kitchen pantry for a rawhide chew. He returned to the front door, licking his chops. Take that, cat.

Resisting the urge to go back to bed, I popped a tea pod into my Keurig. After stirring a generous helping of milk and a squirt of honey into my mug, I sat down at the kitchen table. I wrote down today's to do's on the legal pad in front of me while I sipped my hot tea. At the top of the list was some surveillance work for the insurance company's case followed by a visit to

Chantal. I hoped I could wrap the insurance work up quickly so I could focus exclusively on finding Peg's killer.

***

Parking across the street from the duplex where the target lived, I pulled out the good digital camera that I used for surveillance and my notepad. I took a couple of test shots and reviewed them. Angle was good. The target, a female hairdresser in her forties, had been in a car accident. She was suing the insured for lost wages and emotional trauma. She had not shown up for work for two weeks. The doctor she saw had a reputation for insurance scams.

I hated doing surveillance work. To start, I couldn't use my Volvo. Way too obvious. I either had to borrow Gunner's van or rent a nondescript vehicle. Gunner needed the van, so I'd rented a black Honda Accord. I always requested leather seats, but they didn't have anything available. The velour seats felt dirty and the combination of stale smoke and the Lysol I sprayed on the inside was nauseating. I had the windows slightly cracked to help. Every time I cranked the a/c up high, the windows misted over so I was stuck with wiping away beads of perspiration from my neck every five minutes. Two-thirds of the time surveillance was a big fat waste of time. Then there was the other third where you gleaned useful information, or better yet received a big break in the case. To make the situation even worse, I didn't dare drink anything. I learned that lesson early on when I took a pee break and missed the two minutes of action after four hours of waiting.

As I waited, I thought about the incredible ending to the previous evening. Was the kiss a mistake brought on by too much alcohol? Did Brad regret it? Just remembering that kiss woke up the butterflies again.

A car pulling into the duplex driveway interrupted my thoughts. A woman with long brown hair exited the car and rang the hairdresser's doorbell. Zooming in with my camera, I snapped a couple of shots. She had on a bright orange shirt and jeans. I managed to capture the street address in the photos as well. I took another picture of the license plate on her car. Unfortunately, I didn't get a good shot of whoever was behind the door when it opened. About an hour later, an older woman in a lime green dress with salt and pepper hair rang the doorbell and the woman in orange walked out. Her hair had been cut into a flattering bob cut. Snap, snap, snap. I took more pictures, including one of her getting into her car and another of the older woman's license plate. Forty-five minutes later, the older woman exited, her hair now shiny black. When the hairdresser walked out with a bag of trash and no neck brace, I had what I needed.

Back at the office, I called my friend at the DMV. Sure, it was Sunday, but I'd done some surveillance work on her ex when I worked for BridgePoint. We became friends, and she never minded doing me a favor. She logged in from home and checked the license plates. In no time, I had names, numbers, and addresses. We agreed to hook up for lunch soon.

I placed a phone call to the first woman, Tanya, claiming the hairdresser had given me her name as a reference. Tanya gave her great accolades and said she was so happy Josie was working out of her house now. "In fact, I just got a new bob cut today and I love it."

Total score.

Satisfied that I had everything I needed, I typed up the report, pasting in the better digital photos. I emailed the document to the insurance company, along with an invoice for the balance due.

After dropping off the rental car and picking up my Volvo, I headed for Chantal's apartment along Meeting Street. I dreaded this encounter. I'd set up the meeting with her two days ago under the guise of having information about Peg's estate. Underhanded, I know, but it was the only way to guarantee she would meet with me, and maybe, if I was lucky, she'd be half-sober. I knocked several times before she came to the door. She was obviously nursing a hangover. Her eyes were bloodshot, and she winced at the bright sun streaming through the open door.

"Thanks for letting me come over." Stepping inside, I scanned the room. A thin layer of dust coated the entry table, but otherwise the space was tidy.

"Come in Liz. Can I get you a drink? Coffee, iced tea, a martini?"

Hallelujah, she wasn't slurring her words. "Just some water would be nice, thanks, Chantal." I sat on her slate gray suede couch that was framed by black-and-cream houndstooth club chairs. Pillows covered in identical fabric were layered on the couch. A sheepskin area rug sat underneath a long gray reclaimed-wood coffee table.

While Chantal fixed a martini for herself and a water for me, I admired the artwork on the opposite wall.

Returning, she handed me a glass and sat in one of the club chairs.

After sipping my water, I asked, "Did Peg decorate this place?"

"No. She isn't the only one with talent you know."

Yikes, not a good start. "I was just admiring your artwork. I'm not usually a fan of abstract art, but I love it. Who's the artist?"

"That would be me."

"They're fantastic. Are they oils?" There were three large unframed canvases on the wall. Swirls and layering of purples, creams, grays, and black created a sense of progressive movement.

"Yes, oils. C'mon, Liz. I don't want to be surprised at the reading of the will. What do you know about Peg's estate? Am I finally free of my parents' purse strings?"

She said it with such bitterness, I cringed. Didn't she feel any grief? Was it honestly all about the money? "You are an amazingly talented artist," I replied, avoiding the subject and trying to keep my anger in check.

"Let's just say my art phase happened before my drunken one. Cut to the chase Liz, did Peg take care of her little sis or not?" She pursed her lips and narrowed her eyes.

I wanted to scream at her. Instead, I said, "Why don't you tell me about the last time you saw her?"

She took a big swig of her martini. "So, this is how it works? I give you information and in exchange, you give me information. Fine. The last time I saw my sister was at the yacht club about two weeks ago."

A few moments of silence passed, and her eyes misted up as she remembered. "For once I felt she was truly happy to see me."

Chantal was striking in ways that differed from Peg. She had auburn hair and almond-shaped brown eyes set in a face that was more handsome than pretty. Bitterness and too much alcohol had etched deep lines around her lips and eyes.

"What happened?" I studied her closely as she answered.

"Stupid Alex was there with his latest girlfriend. And, once again, he made Peg feel like shit. She sat down at the bar and had a martini with me. Peg is always … was always prepared." She took another big swallow of her drink and continued, "But she didn't have any Kleenex on her that day. For once, I was able to give her something. Usually, it's the other way around." She sighed. "You know I've thought about that day over and over. It was the best exchange we've had in a long time. I know I'm a mess, Liz, but I really did love my sister. I wish our relationship had been better."

I started empathizing with her. However, I knew from Peg's stories how manipulative this woman could be. Was this an act? My gut said Chantal was being real for once. Perhaps losing the sister she felt so inferior to for so long had jolted her into reflecting on her own life. Maybe the negative attention was finally getting old.

"Are you OK with a few more questions?" I asked.

Sitting up taller, she sneered, "Like you care. Go ahead."

"What were you doing the night Peg died?"

"My usual. I went to the tavern on the corner. Friday night is steak night. I hung around until about eleven with the regulars. Came home, fixed a drink, and fell asleep on the couch. Woke up to the news about Peg and twenty missed calls."

More likely passed out on the couch, but OK.

"So, I told you, now you tell me … did my sis leave me any money or not?"

"I don't know for sure. We talked about you before one of her appointments with her lawyer about the will. Peg struggled with what to leave you. She wanted you to get better, healthier. She talked about making whatever she left you contingent on you spending one year in a rehab facility." Although vague, I hoped my response would satisfy her.

"Isn't that peachy?" Chantal slapped the arm of the chair, "Still trying to control me from her grave. You know everyone thought I'd be the one to go first and look at me. I'm still here. Peg's not. I'm done now. You can let yourself out."

Shock pinned me to my seat for a moment, then I stood. "I'm sorry."

"Whatever."

Chantal remained seated as I let myself out of her apartment. Outside, walking back to my car, I felt more confused than ever. I couldn't dismiss the fact that she had a motive, and her alibi was iffy at best. Yet, despite the chip on her shoulder, I believed that she truly loved her sister. My gut said to cross her off the list. However, my mind said she was still a viable suspect. She could've gone to Peg's that night. And she knew her sister would welcome her in.

Motive and a weak alibi.

Back in my home office, I placed a few phone calls, starting with Barbie, the scorned client. She answered the phone breathless as if she just finished a workout. She was more than happy to chat and speculate about who killed Peg. I could tell she was a professional gossip. Barbie had very few nice things to say about Peg. Obviously, she still carried a grudge about Peg and Lou not finishing the decorating job. She bragged about her home being featured in last November's *Southern Living*. Barbie claimed she and her husband were at an overnight gala the night of Peg's death that concluded with a breakfast of caviar and Eggs Benedict around six a.m. Easy enough to check out.

Switching gears, I pulled out my index cards and added notes. Then I turned on my computer and googled La Maison d' Bjorn and CM Partners Ltd. The website for La Maison d'Bjorn consisted of a landing page with a picture of the storefront and a contact page. Nothing returned from my search on CM Partners, not even formation documents. I found a few interviews with Bjorn about the antique business. After seeing his picture, I could understand Peg's attraction to him. I added what little I'd learned to my notes and moved on.

I had some more checking to do on Barbie, but she was a long shot. I sent her a text thanking her for her time and mentioned I'd love to see her beautiful home. Barbie called back in less than a minute.

"I got your text. I thought it would be easier to coordinate a time over the phone. My schedule's kind of tight. I could squeeze you in on Monday afternoon around one-thirty before my massage."

We agreed on the time, and she gave me directions to her gated community. She promised to give the security guards a heads up that I was coming. I did a search on the gala she'd attended the night Peg was killed. I knew the coordinator, who was a friend of Peg's. Placing a quick call to her, she confirmed Barbie and her husband were at the gala that awful night. Meeting Barbie was probably a waste of time, but I couldn't resist the temptation to meet a real 'Barbie' in person.

A big gap in my investigation was information about the boyfriend, Bjorn. My notes on him were sparse. Hopefully, a quick trip to Paris would provide some helpful material. Technically, I wasn't supposed to leave town, but I needed to meet Bjorn. Peg would definitely approve of my visit to one of her favorite places. I could leave the day after the reading of the will. Honestly, a few days away would do me some good. Using my miles to splurge on a first-class ticket, I booked a flight and printed off my itinerary. I put the printout on the desk in the kitchen along with a post-it reminder to contact Bjorn. Brad pinged me with a text thanking me for dinner last night. I'd been wondering when I'd hear from him again.

Three o'clock. I had three hours before the game night. Just enough time for a B&E into Bruce's place.

Chapter 16

I unlatched the back gate. No one would think twice about me checking on Buddy. Bruce had an alarm system, but I knew he didn't use it. He'd set it off accidentally several times, costing himself a small fortune in fees for the false alarms. The non-existent blinking red light confirmed it wasn't on. I easily picked the lock on the back door. Buddy bounded in before me through the doggy door.

Bruce's kitchen sink was full of dirty dishes. The coffee pot was half-full, but off. The refrigerator was packed with to-go containers, and the freezer was stuffed with microwave dinners. Moving on to the living area, I checked the closet underneath the stairs. Sure enough, I found a baseball bat. Dusting the handle, I lifted the prints and placed them in an envelope. The closet also contained luggage, a couple of basketballs, a set of little-used golf clubs, a vacuum cleaner, a couple of brooms, and cleaning supplies.

Bruce's floor plan varied from mine. The office was downstairs and all the bedrooms were upstairs. Closing the closet door, I headed toward his office. Flipping on his computer, I plugged my thumb drive with the password detector program into the portal. In less than a minute, I had the password, Bruce@home. People could be so unimaginative. His screensaver flashed on with about half a dozen changing pictures. The first three were of his kids. The fourth one was Buddy begging for a treat. The next one, taken at a neighborhood party, included everyone in the community. It was one of those group selfies. I cringed at my goofy smile. The last was from the same party. I remembered Bruce asking Cassie to take it. Peg and I were in the center. Bruce was on the other side of Peg, and Lou on the other side of me. Studying the four of us, I sighed at the memory. The next picture was an older Black couple, Bruce's parents? The last was a group picture of staff from the hospital.

After poking around in Bruce's electronic files, I moved on to his paper files. He had a long wooden credenza behind his desk. Fortunately, his files were fairly organized. Tax returns, warranties, a file for each of the kids, and divorce papers. Pulling out the file titled "work" I flipped through the pages. I found a letter from Mercy Hospital in Illinois. The letter summarized the results of an investigation clearing him from a wrongful death accusation. During an emergency appendectomy, Bruce's patient, a twenty-year-old female, had gone into cardiac arrest. The letter ended with a clause stating he was clear to return to work. Taking a picture with my phone, I glimpsed at the time. An hour had passed. Time to explore the upstairs.

The second floor contained three bedrooms. A pink and white one, obviously for his daughter, and a room filled with sports pennants and posters for his son. I skipped the kids' bedrooms and focused on the master.

Bruce's bedroom was an organized mess. The bed was unmade. A week's worth of clothes were carefully laid over a chaise in the corner. Stacks of medical journals sat on the nightstand by the bed. A half-empty bottle of a lemon-lime sports drink perched on top. My search of the nightstand drawers turned up nothing of interest. He had a whole drawer dedicated to orphan socks. Nothing under the bed other than a bunch of dust bunnies.

Entering the bathroom, I noticed the high-end man products. Bruce was meticulous about his appearance. Wet towels were in a pile on the floor. Otherwise, the bathroom was clean. Moving on to the closet, I stumbled over a sea of tennis shoes. He owned at least twenty pairs. His scrubs hung neatly on one side of the closet. His dress and casual clothes hung on the other side. Searching pockets, I found spare change, pieces of paper with phone numbers, and a couple of business cards. I unfolded a small ladder that I found in the corner of the closet and started searching the top shelves. There were a couple of empty backpacks. A stack of *Playboy* magazines was hidden underneath a shoebox filled with extra shoelaces. Placing the small ladder back in place, I spotted a garbage bag in the far corner. Opening it up, I was disappointed to find a bunch of worn tennis shoes. The alarm on my phone went off. Five o'clock—time to go home.

Forty-five minutes after I returned home, there was a loud rap on my front door. Bruce stood rigid with Buddy in one arm and a paper bag in the other. I was tempted to ignore him. However, I was pretty sure he saw me through the window.

"Hi Bruce, Buddy, come in."

Bruce set Buddy down, and the dogs headed for the Duke's toy basket.

"She's haunting me!" Bruce's face was ashen and his hands were shaking.

"What are you talking about?"

"It's Peg. She's haunting me. I could smell her perfume

in the house when I came home. Do you think it's because I found her first?"

I'd forgotten what a sensitive nose Bruce had. When we walked the dogs, he could smell if someone hadn't picked up poop from yards away.

"I don't think so." I rubbed my chin. "Could it be your imagination? I know this has been a stressful time."

Bruce crossed his arms. "I'm not imagining things."

"OK." I hesitated and then asked, "Did you ever talk to the therapist at work?"

"That's why I'm here. Can you watch Buddy tonight? I'm going to stay at the hotel by the hospital. I'm totally freaked out. I can't stay at my place. Seeing the therapist tomorrow morning."

"Of course. Duke will be excited." It was the least I could do after scaring the man half to death. I put my arm around him, trying to offer some comfort. "Are you OK?"

Bruce took a deep breath, "Yeah, I will be. I think it's all caught up with me. Maybe I'll take a couple of days off soon. Get some rest. Thanks for watching Buddy for me."

"Happy to. But I can only do two nights. I'm headed out of town on Wednesday."

Bruce gave me a quizzical look. "Out of town? I thought you weren't allowed to leave?"

Remembering the conversation from our walk, I lied through my teeth, "Headed to Columbia for a few nights to get away. I'm allowed to do that." Luckily, Duke wasn't paying attention; he was too enamored with Buddy to give a yip.

"Do you need me to watch Duke while you're gone?" Bruce asked.

"Nah. He's coming with me. Thanks though."

Handing over the paper bag, Bruce said, "I brought Buddy's food, his treats, and his leash. It'll only be one night. I just need to pull myself back together. Thanks for doing this."

I felt guilty, but once he left, I couldn't stop giggling. The look on Bruce's face after believing his house was haunted was priceless.

***

Cassie opened the door, and I handed her a bouquet of daisies and a bottle of chardonnay. She wore an oversized purple blouse and white capris. Her violet eyes twinkled. "Come in. You're the last to arrive."

Whereas Lou and Peg's homes looked like they could be featured in *Architectural Digest*, Cassie's home would likely be found in *Country Living*. Plaid fabrics, needlepoint pillows, cross-stitch pictures, and hand-braided rugs completed the decor. As usual, everyone congregated in the kitchen.

A spread of crackers, cheeses, olives, and raw veggies filled the island countertop. A pot of seafood gumbo simmered on the stove. I poured myself a glass of wine and joined the gathering.

"The security guys came today. Security system is all set," Linda said. "I feel so much safer."

"Can I get the name of the company you used?" Maria asked.

"Me too," Gwen chimed in. She sighed, "I sure wish Peg was here with us."

We were all quiet for a few minutes, and I felt the absence of her presence.

Breaking the silence, Maria asked, "Liz, have you found out anything new?" She hesitated briefly before continuing. "Was it a break-in?"

"No," Cassie answered for me. "The police said there were no signs of a break-in." She prided herself on being the first to know the neighborhood news. Cassie began ladling gumbo into bowls. "Now, grab a bowl of gumbo and some salad. Let's get started."

"Sassy Cassie is the boss," I whispered to Gwen.

A Scrabble board sat waiting in the middle of the round pine table in the breakfast nook. If Peg were here, we would have two separate games going. Instead, a tile holder from another game had been borrowed so the five of us could sit together.

Cassie went first, with the word "jumper." I played "mystery" seven letters. "So, Cassie, how did you find out there wasn't a break-in?" I asked as she tallied up the points.

Cassie blushed. "That nice officer, Sam, asked me out to dinner."

"You went on a date with Sam?" I asked in disbelief.

"Two dates. We also went to see a movie. I want to invite him over for dinner. He's such a gentleman. What do you think, Liz? I've never dated a policeman before."

Astonished that Cassie called Sam nice and a gentleman, I nearly choked on my wine. Were we talking about the same Sam? "This is the Sam that was at Lou's place the morning of Peg's death?"

"Yes, hon. What do you think?"

Gwen interrupted our conversation. "Trouble. Triple word, thirty-four points."

Trouble about summed up my thoughts on Sam, but I didn't want to spoil Cassie's fun.

"If you cook for him, you're guaranteed a friend for life," I said instead. It was an honest answer.

Linda played "dibbles" off Gwen's "b" and practically jumped out of her chair. "Seven letters, triple word." She stood up and did a little happy dance.

Wow. One hundred-plus points.

"You guys are a tough crowd." Maria tapped her fingers on the table as she contemplated her tiles.

My mind wandered to our last game night, and my heart did a little twist. Peg loved game night. We'd been playing a competitive game of Pictionary with Peg, Linda, and Cassie on one team. Me, Maria, and Gwen on the other. I thought it would be fun to have a Mexican theme, so we had build-your-own tacos and frozen margaritas. I forgot Gwen couldn't handle hard liquor. I reflected back on that night.

Peg was drawing a man and woman hugging when Gwen flipped. "I saw you hugging Nick at the Christmas party," she hissed at Peg.

"So what Gwen, this is the South everybody hugs." Peg shrugged. Cassie snatched Gwen's margarita glass and replaced it with a bottle of water from the kitchen.

"I see the way he looks at you." Gwen crossed her arms and glared at Peg.

Help, Peg silently mouthed at me.

"Gwen, will you help me bring the chips and queso from the kitchen? I don't know about y'all, but I have the munchies."

That seemed to snap Gwen back to her normal self. After fetching the snacks from the kitchen, we continued the game without incident.

Returning to the present, I noticed that Gwen was drinking wine tonight. Thank God.

Maria played ex and ox with the x on a triple letter square.

"Has anyone seen Tina lately? I spent hours searching for her the other day with no luck," I said.

Cassie shook her head. Gwen said, "I saw her about two weeks ago. She was at Peg's."

Maria asked, "Who's Tina?"

Linda explained who she was, then finished with, "I haven't seen her lately either."

"Peg looked after her," I added. "I'd like for one of us to break the news to Tina about Peg's death. I'd hate for her to hear it on the streets. Let me know if you see her." I considered my next move.

Gwen grinned and her eyes lit up, "Guess who I saw at Liz's last night."

I rolled my eyes and tried to derail the direction of this conversation. "It was just Peg's friend, Brad. I had him over for dinner. I needed to ask him a few questions. Don't make a big deal out of it Gwen."

"Uh-huh. The same Brad who sent her a gorgeous flower arrangement … a romance is budding." Gwen winked.

"Ooooh, sounds juicy Liz, do tell," Linda added.

"Right now, nothing of note. But if there ever is, y'all will be the first to know." Good thing Duke wasn't around to yip. Cassie finally played her word, and then I took my turn.

Three games later, we called it a night. Maria ended up winning three of the four games after losing the first one to Linda.

It had been a long day and I had another B&E on the agenda for tomorrow.

Chapter 17

My neighbor, Nick, knocked on my door at eight a.m. sharp. "Come in. I'll fix you a cup of coffee."

"I can't stay. I need a favor. What's Buddy doing here?" Nick bent down and patted Buddy's head before turning his attention to Duke.

"Bruce needed me to watch him for a night. What's up?"

"I have to go out of town for the night. Will you check on Gwen for me? I'm worried about her. Not a problem if you can't do it. I asked Cassie, too." He ran his fingers through his thick white hair.

"Of course. Is she alright? She seemed fine last night."

"She's still a mess over Peg's death. Doesn't like to be alone for long. Thanks, Liz, I owe you one."

Once Nick left, I shot Lou a quick text asking if he wanted to join me for a coffee before he hit the road. I needed to confirm he was heading out of town. He replied within minutes.

Join me for coffee?

Sure, give me 15.

K.

I pulled the spare key to his place out of the kitchen drawer and slipped it into my pocket. Lou had given it to me several years ago so that I could water his plants when he was out of town. I straightened the downstairs while waiting for his arrival. True to his word, Lou arrived fifteen minutes later. Unlocking the door, I motioned him inside.

"What's Buddy doing here?" he asked.

I answered for the second time this morning, then nodded his way. "You look dapper." Lou was dressed in white jeans and a black V-neck T-shirt.

"Thanks. Now, where's that coffee?"

Standing around the kitchen island, Lou sipped his coffee while I nursed my hot tea.

"So, who's the client?" I asked.

"A doctor and her husband. They're redoing their master bedroom and bath."

Duke yipped. Puzzled, I continued "And you're headed to Colombia?"

"Yeah." No yip from Duke. At least that part rang true. "By the way, thanks for dinner the other night. It felt good to laugh and share memories of our Peg. And the casserole was delish. Can I get the recipe?"

"Sure." I fetched the recipe out of my cupboard and ran upstairs to make a quick copy.

Back downstairs, I handed the recipe to Lou then said, "I'm dreading tomorrow. Do you have any idea what Peg put in her will?"

"Only what was in our partnership agreement. You?" Duke yipped.

Hmm. Why would he lie? I shook my head. "I don't even know why they invited me to the reading. Are you sure you don't know the details of her will?"

"No, doll. Why do you ask?" Another yip from Duke. He was definitely lying.

"What's up with Duke?"

"He hasn't had his breakfast yet." Duke yipped again. I gave both Duke and Buddy a treat.

Once the dogs were settled, I turned my attention back to Lou. "About the will. It just seems like she would have shared a little about it with one of us. Especially you as a partner."

Lou quickly put his coffee cup down. "Gotta run."

"So soon?"

"Yeah. You want to ride to the reading together tomorrow?"

"Can't. Meeting Jenny for lunch beforehand."

Lou air-kissed my cheeks. "Thanks for the coffee and the recipe. See you later."

I waited thirty minutes, just long enough to ensure he didn't return because he forgot something. I put on a ball cap and some sunglasses, not much of a disguise. Our neighbors wouldn't think twice about me walking into Lou's place and if anyone mentioned it, I'd deal with the questions then. Once the coast cleared, I walked across the street and slipped the key in his door.

I safely had at least three hours, but I hoped it wouldn't take that long. I started in the master bedroom and worked my way through each room ending with the garage. Walking into Lou's closet, I was not surprised to discover that it was meticulously arranged. Shirts hung by type and by color all on matching hangers, and he had more shoes than I did. I felt around in the pockets of his jackets, coming up empty. I ran my hand along the top shelf of the closet, which I could barely reach. Nothing there. Not even dust.

He'd made the bed. I searched under the pillows, under the bed, and under the mattress. Nothing but luggage under the bed. Opening the nightstand drawer, I discovered a worn leather journal. Sitting on the bed, I flipped to two weeks before Peg's murder and began reading.

The entries described his frustrations and struggles with being gay. He was attracted to a guy at the coffee shop he frequents, but he'd had bad experiences with approaching someone directly. He'd been observing him, trying to determine if the guy might also be gay. He emphasized several times he needed to break it off with Joe. Someone was bound to find out, and that would be trouble for both of them.

Who was Joe? Lou hadn't mentioned him to me.

He wrote about the disagreement with Peg over Bjorn and his reservations about him. Then he ranted for a full page about a discussion he'd with Peg about the types of clients they have. She liked the residential clients, and he preferred the commercial side. He wanted to focus on restaurants and hotels.

' … I can't understand why Peg won't listen to me,' he wrote. 'She can be so stubborn. The commercial side is so much easier and less high maintenance than all of her rich friends and family. I know we could make a go of it. She won't even consider it. Says they are our bread and butter, blah, blah, blah. I think she's afraid to rock the boat. Sometimes, I wonder if it would be easier to go into business for myself.'

Interesting, tidbit of information.

Over the next few pages were entries about various clients and ideas for several projects. The following day's entry contained additional ideas after he'd shared his thoughts with Peg.

Ouch. An entry about me. Lou got miffed when I interrupted them having a cocktail at Peg's house. I remembered that night. There was a new restaurant I wanted to try, so I'd popped over after walking Duke to see if Peg wanted to go. They were in the midst of putting together a big proposal for a renovation of a hotel downtown. He resented the intrusion. In all fairness, I didn't know they were having a meeting, and I did ask if he wanted to join us.

No entry for the morning of Peg's murder. Not a surprise. That day was crazy. The following day's pages were filled with agony, grief, and musings about how to handle the business. Should he bring in another partner? Was now the time to wean off the residential side and focus on the commercial industry? Was there enough cash to get through the months ahead? What would he do if what happened in college resurfaced? And when should he go to Paris to handle the business there?

He wondered who could have possibly killed her. He even listed my name with a question mark. He also wrote that he worried about me and was concerned about my safety, which was touching.

The entry for this morning was interesting. ... 'Headed to see Joe. Olivia is working. I don't know how long we can continue this. The job's been finished for over a month. Maybe I'll finally break it off today ... or maybe not.'

That explained one of Duke's yips. Tucking the journal back into the drawer, I moved on to the study.

Lou's study was decorated with a hunting theme. I loved the room. The wood-paneled walls melted into a floor-to-ceiling bookcase. Filled with hardback books in every color and genre, it was like a mini-library. A large wooden desk sat atop a dark green and gold oriental rug. A dark green leather chair was anchored behind it. Prints of hunting dogs hung on the walls. Natural light poured through two windows with a view of the water. I narrowed the openings on the wooden blinds just in case someone walked by.

Lou did indeed suck at filing. He had an overflowing inbox filled with bills, paperwork, and torn-out decorating articles and pictures. Post-It notes were everywhere. One, in particular, caught my attention. Book flight to Paris. No computer. He must've taken his laptop with him. The study closet contained a couple of metal filing cabinets filled with tax returns, warranties, titles, etc. The files had no particular order to them, the paperwork half haphazardly shoved into each one. The top shelves of the closet were filled with stacks of photo books and decorating magazines.

Reopening the wooden blinds, I moved on to my second favorite room, the kitchen. Lou's kitchen was decorated in shades of ivory and gray. Ivory wooden cabinets were framed with gorgeous carved molding. Gleaming granite countertops in gray and ivory hues. A large kitchen island. Stainless steel appliances. Slate gray floor. A distressed round pedestal table was surrounded by open-backed chairs with cushions covered in gray and cream stripes. Two sparkling chandeliers caught the sunlight. Not a single dish in the sink, and the coffee pot contained no remnants of this morning's brew.

Two hours later, I returned home feeling somewhat wiser, but terribly guilty about snooping on a friend. I found nothing to indicate he murdered Peg and no copy of the will. The only item of note was the speculation about launching his own business. And then, there was the question of Joe.

I needed to talk through what I'd learned so far. Picking up the phone, I called Gunner.

"Yo, Liz, what's up?" Gunner asked.

"I'm feeling guilty about breaking into two neighbors' houses," I replied.

"Which ones?"

"Lou and Bruce."

"What'd you find?"

I described my tour through each of their homes and shared what I discovered about Bruce's medical license. Gunner said, "Sometimes what you don't find is as important as what you do."

That did little to ease my guilt and frustration. "You have any news for me?" I asked.

"Cameras picked up a few people on the street the night Peg was killed. A couple of unidentified drunk kids around midnight. A couple of night ladies and that homeless girl, Tina, around one."

Night ladies was Gunner's lingo for a hooker.

"Did you recognize any of the ladies?" I put a special emphasis on the last word and Gunner chuckled.

"Actually I did." He rattled off a couple of names and I jotted them down. I recognized one of the names, Sabrina. She'd helped me out on a domestic case a few years ago.

"Do you mind seeing what you can find out from the ladies? Maybe one of them saw something or could help me find Tina."

"You got it."

"Thanks, Gunner."

"You take care of yourself kid."

As soon as I hung up the phone, it buzzed again. "Hi, Brad."

"Thanks for dinner the other night. I meant to call sooner. It's been a little crazy helping Ian and Irene get the house ready for the reading tomorrow. Plus trying to run a business remotely."

"No worries. It was my pleasure." My heart sped up, wondering if he'd mention the kiss.

After an awkward pause, he said, "I'd like to see you again. Just you and me."

I hesitated before answering, "I'd like that too."

"Let's talk tomorrow and figure out details."

Hanging up the phone, I turned to Duke and said, "What have we gotten ourselves into?"

Chapter 18

After walking the dogs, I went next door to check on Gwen. She opened the door before I knocked.

"Come in, Liz. Nick said you might stop by. Honestly, it's not necessary, but I appreciate the company. I was just making myself a ham salad sandwich. Would you like one?"

I couldn't remember the last time I'd eaten ham salad. "That sounds delicious."

We walked into the kitchen where she finished the preparations, then handed me a plate with the sandwich, chips, and a dill pickle, along with a bottle of water. We sat down at their glass-top kitchen table. Sun streamed through the bay window casting rainbow prisms of light through the glass.

"Last night was fun. Maria sure can play," I said.

"Hrmph, luck." She wiped the corner of her mouth with a napkin.

"Gwen, did you and Peg have words the week before she died?"

"I feel so terrible. It was our last conversation." She blew her nose in her napkin. "Peg gave Nick an expensive bottle of Scotch she bought at an auction. I didn't think it was proper. Told her if she had something to give to Nick, she should give it through me."

"What did Peg say?"

"At first she told me I was being silly. But in the end, she agreed."

We both sat silently for several minutes before Gwen said, "I saw you breaking into Lou's."

I sat back in my chair. How would I get her to keep this bit of information to herself? "I wasn't breaking in. I have a key."

"So, he asked you to check his place?" Her hazel eyes glared at me.

"No. Listen, Gwen, we all want this murder solved. I know you'll feel safer once Peg's killer is brought to justice."

Her hand shook as she lifted the water bottle to her lips. "Do you think Lou did it?"

"Not at all. As her business partner and friend, he was close to her. I just thought I might find a clue."

"Did you?"

I shook my head.

Gwen pointed a shaking finger at me. "Well. I don't think that's right going into someone's house without their permission. What's to stop you from coming in ours and snooping around?"

"I've only been investigating people who are possible suspects. You and Nick are not on that list." Again, I wondered if I should add her. Gwen's prints were in the system but she could've worn gloves. Nah, I couldn't picture her touching a gun.

"Hrmph." Gwen took another swallow of her water.

"Can we please keep this between the two of us?"

"Why? You need to be stopped. You can't just go into people's houses."

I hated to bring up what I knew about her past, but she left me no choice. I needed to guarantee her silence. "I ran a background check on you. Shoplifting?" I gave her a stern look.

Gwen's mouth formed an 'O,' and she took in a sharp breath. The room fell silent for several minutes before she spoke in a soft voice, "I suffer from anxiety. Taking things used to be the way I dealt with it. The thrill of getting away with it took away the anxiety, temporarily. Until I got caught. But I never took any valuable items. Just stupid stuff. Like a candy bar or a pair of cheap earrings." She sighed, "After I was caught, I paid everything back as part of my probation. Then, Nick got me in therapy, and I take anti-anxiety meds. I haven't shoplifted in years. Please don't tell anyone, Liz."

"How about we make a deal? You don't tell, and I won't tell."

Gwen leaned back in her chair and crossed her arms. "OK."

I felt bad about blackmailing her. We ate the rest of our sandwiches in silence. I left as soon as I was convinced that she wasn't going to have a major anxiety attack.

***

I stopped at the entrance to Barbie's neighborhood and rolled down the car window. A husky male security guard checked my name off a list and opened the gate. Driving to the end of the cul-de-sac, I was astonished at the size of the homes. A white colonial with black shutters and a cherry red door, Barbie's home sat on at least half an acre. Framed with hot-pink azaleas, the house sprawled across most of the lot. A large magnolia tree was in full bloom. I inhaled the scent as I rang the bell. A young woman in her mid-twenties opened the door. Her long black hair was pulled back in a ponytail. She had beautiful gray eyes that sparkled on a make-up-free freckled face. Surely, this wasn't Barbie.

I heard Barbie's voice in the background. "Lydia, is that Liz? Bring her to the living room. We'll start there."

Of course, Barbie didn't answer her own door. Lydia introduced herself as Barbie's maid and escorted me to the living room. The space opened up to two stories, the walls and columns painted a dove gray. A fire crackled in the marble fireplace even though it was eighty-five degrees outside. Floor-to-ceiling windows were framed by heavy marshmallow-colored drapes. The spotless furniture appeared as if it had been taken directly off the showroom floor and moved into the space. A tall vase of fresh flowers sat in the center of the coffee table.

Barbie hugged me as if we had known each other all of our lives. "Liz, I'm so glad you could come. What would you like to drink?"

Barbie looked just like I'd imagined. Long bleached blonde hair tumbled past her shoulders. Her lips were unnaturally puffy and her face barely moved when she smiled, most likely a result of some type of surgical injection. She had blue eyes framed by well-done fake lashes. She had a figure to die for, obviously not entirely the result of a rigorous workout routine. "I'd love an iced tea," I responded.

"Lydia, an iced tea for Liz and another mimosa for me."

The maid left, returning a few minutes later, balancing a silver tray with our drinks. Picking up our glasses, we began our tour. The dining room had a long ebony table that seated at least twenty people. Next, Barbie led the way into a huge game room with a simulated golf practice area, a billiard table, card tables, and a full bar. The exercise room was three times the size of our community fitness center and had a steam room.

As we went from room to room, Barbie entertained me with stories from various parties and events they hosted. In between telling stories, she pumped me for information about Peg's murder. She had a morbid sense of curiosity, and she didn't offer her condolences. I could tell she was concocting a tale to tell at her next party.

"Who do you think did it, Liz?" Barbie glanced at her phone and tapped a quick reply to a message.

"It's early in the investigation." I wasn't about to give her the next party story.

"Had to be either Lou or Alex. Probably Lou. Surely you have some idea."

"Why Alex or Lou?" I asked.

"Lou gets the business. Easy peasy. Alex? Maybe a crime of passion. Don't know if it broke his heart when they split. Divorce can be nasty."

I could tell she spoke from experience. I also sensed she still carried a grudge against Lou. Fortunately, her phone rang with a call she 'had to take,' and it was easy enough to change the subject when she finished.

By the time we completed the tour, my ears burned with the neighborhood gossip, and my feet hurt from walking. I wished I'd worn my sneakers. We placed our empty glasses back on the tray.

"Thank you for your time."

"You're so welcome." She glanced at her phone. "Perfect timing. My masseuse should be here any minute." She personally walked me to the door. I hoped she didn't consider me her new best friend.

As I made my way out the door, a tall well-toned guy walked up the driveway.

"There he is." Barbie flew out the door to hug him. "Bye, Liz. Lunch soon?" She gave me a little wave while entangled in the burly man's arms.

"Bye," I replied without answering her question, happy to be exiting Barbie-world.

***

The doorbell rang and Buddy started jumping up and down. It was Bruce. His face seemed noticeably more relaxed.

"Buddy!" Bruce bent down and picked him up. Buddy licked Bruce's face, his tail wagging a hundred miles an hour.

"He missed you," I said.

"Thanks for watching him."

"You look refreshed."

"I feel a lot better. The therapist helped. Being gone and not so close to where it all happened helped too. I can't thank you enough."

"What are friends for?" I responded.

Poor Duke sat by the door for ten minutes after his pal left.

***

Since I'd be out of town this coming Friday and not able to make our lunch date, Jenny and I agreed to meet at George's Grill in Mount Pleasant before the reading of the will. About a twenty-minute drive from Charleston, the town was an easy commute and a popular place for families to put down roots. The reading would take place at four o'clock at Ian and Irene's home in the country club community nearby. I arrived a few minutes late for lunch as it took me forever to select an outfit. I finally settled on a black halter-neck sundress with a wide coral belt and black espadrilles with a slight heel. I opted for simple jewelry, a gold necklace and gold hoop earrings.

When I walked into the restaurant, Jenny gave me a big smile, "You look fantastic,"

"Thanks. You look great, too." Jenny wore a black and turquoise patterned sheath dress with sandals and turquoise Kendra Scott earrings. We were both of the same Southern mindset. When in doubt, dress up, not down.

"Sorry I'm late," I said.

"No worries. I've been studying the menu. The food looks amazing. I can't decide if I want a salad or one of the seafood dishes. The fried shrimp looks good. But knowing Aunt Irene, she'll have a lot of food, so maybe I'll get a salad."

She set the menu down and I noticed her new turquoise nails. "I see Aunt Jane struck." I chuckled.

Jenny held her hand up. "Yep. They're nice but I can't quite get used to them."

The waitress arrived and we both decided on the mahi-mahi salad. A bloody mary sounded tempting, but instead, I ordered a glass of iced tea with a splash of sweet tea.

"I'm nervous about this afternoon. I've never been to a reading of a will before. Do you know who else will be there?" I didn't admit the other reason my nerves were jumping. The thought of seeing Brad had the butterflies working overtime.

"Other than family, no. I called Aunt Irene yesterday to find out if I could bring a dish. She said there'll be about thirty people. She's having the club cater it. What picture did you bring?"

"It's a series of pictures. Peg and I were at a party and the hosts had one of those photo booths. We had a blast making all kinds of silly faces for the camera. Those pictures remind me of all the fun we had together and all the laughs."

"Nice. I can't wait to see them." She took a sip of her water. "How'd dinner go the other night? Did you find out anything new from Brad?"

I blushed and hoped Jenny didn't notice. "Not really. We mostly shared memories of Peg. Lou joined us too. I loved hearing some of the stories Brad and Lou told."

"Liz, are you blushing?" Jenny asked.

"He kissed me," I blurted out.

"Brad?"

"No. Lou, silly. Of course, Brad. I'm a jumble of nerves thinking about seeing him again. We were both a bit tipsy." I still wondered if the alcohol had influenced the kiss.

Jenny clapped her hands together and almost jumped out of her chair. "Oh my gosh. You guys would make the most beautiful couple. He's so gorgeous. Aunt Peg would be thrilled."

"I'm sure it was a mistake brought on by too much wine, but…oh, can he kiss." My cheeks felt warm.

The waitress appeared with our salads, a beautiful presentation of butter lettuce topped with avocado, mango, red onion, and mahi-mahi with a lump of crab meat, finished with a ginger lime dressing. I steered the conversation to the various family members who would be at the reading, fishing for more information on each of them. We speculated about the contents of Peg's will and what she might have left to Chantal.

After lunch, I headed to Ian and Irene's with a heavy heart and a fluttery stomach.

Chapter 19

Ian and Irene's home was on the third hole of the golf course. Fortunately, even though we were in separate cars, Jenny and I arrived at the house at about the same time. I couldn't believe I was so nervous, but I didn't want to walk in by myself. There were a couple of teenage boys directing people where to park. Jenny and I pulled in next to each other and walked up the driveway to the sprawling two-story home. Dressed in a black and white striped dress with fuchsia Kendra Scott accessories, one of the twins greeted people at the front door. Once I realized that Jenny and I were dressed appropriately, I relaxed a little. She gave each of us a hug and took our purses. After asking us to sign in, she double-checked our contact information. Gesturing to the long folding table covered in a black tablecloth she commented. "Mom's making a photo book for everyone. Please place your pictures of Peg over there."

We both signed in and dropped off our photos. While lingering over the various pictures, I sighed. My beautiful friend's life had been cut painfully short. I was grateful that Irene thought of everything, including a big basket filled with packets of mini tissues.

On another table were large manila envelopes with our names and directions not to open until instructed. I grabbed the one with my name and handed Jenny hers. We headed into the combined kitchen and entertainment room where the reading would take place. The French doors opened out onto the pool and deck area. Several chillers were set up underneath the covered deck to battle the heat. The backyard faced north so the sun was not bearing down directly.

Servers milled about the crowd, offering hors d'oeuvres and drinks. If I didn't know better, I'd think I'd arrived at a party. I wasn't hungry, but I gladly took a glass of chardonnay. Jenny nudged me whispering, "There's Brad and he's headed our way." My stomach did a flip-flop. Dressed in a black knit golf shirt and freshly pressed khakis, he looked sharp.

"Liz, Jenny, you guys are beams of sunlight. You both look beautiful." He tenderly kissed my forehead and then kissed Jenny's cheek. "Irene and Ian have been running around like crazy putting this all together. I'm exhausted just watching them."

"Everything's so well organized. They obviously put a lot of thought into it. Any idea why we can't open the envelopes?" I was curious even though I had no point of reference for how these things went.

"No clue," Brad replied. "I just know it took three of us to prep the already sealed envelopes with names and the directive, 'Do NOT Open Until Instructed.'"

Ian walked up greeting each of us. "Sorry girls, I need to borrow Brad."

Jenny nudged me with her elbow. "Oh yeah, he likes you. A lot. I saw the look in his eyes."

"You're imagining things, Jenny." But I secretly hoped she was right.

I scanned the room and waved at Peg's friend, Karen, and her husband, Scott. Lou was engrossed in deep conversation with Peg's oldest brother, Paddy. Liam and Camille were seated on one of the couches. Camille looked exhausted. Chantal was noticeably missing. I was happy that Alex was not amongst the crowd. Jenny headed over to say hello to her dad, and I made my way over to Karen.

"Hi Karen, Scott."

"This is so weird Liz. The last time I was at Irene's house was for Peg's 30th birthday party. A lot of the same people were here then too."

"I guess she and Alex were still married? I'm happy to see he's not here," I said.

"She'd just filed for divorce. He wasn't at the party."

"Where's Chantal?" I asked.

Karen shook her head. "Plastered. Sleeping it off in a back bedroom. I just hope she sleeps through this. Her poor parents have enough to deal with."

The twins weaved through the crowd politely asking everyone to take a seat. Extra folding chairs were set up in the entertainment room, and I sat down next to Jenny. Brad sat down on the other side of me, Lou on the other side of Brad.

"Hello, all. Thank you for coming," Ian said, his deep voice easily carrying through the room. "I know this is a bit unorthodox. Most wills are read in an attorney's office, but Peg wasn't like most people."

That brought a ripple of laughter, and then he continued. "With a family and community the size of ours, Peg attended many funerals. She was explicit about what she wanted in the event of her own death." He took a moment to clear his throat. "Each of you should have a manila envelope. If you don't, please let the girls know and they'll bring you yours. Inside is a copy of the will and a sealed personalized note from Peg."

A buzz filled the room as everyone gasped and whispered to each other. I remembered being at several funerals with Peg. At certain points, she'd comment, "I'd never want that at my funeral, or isn't that a nice touch." She'd hated wakes, but she'd particularly liked the personal touch of leaving letters for loved ones.

"I'll summarize the basic contents of her will. You're welcome to open your packets now and follow along. Peg wanted everyone to hear the same message to stem any gossip. Please refrain from opening the envelope with Peg's note. You are welcome to do so when I finish or at any time of your choosing. I imagine reading her note will be emotional for everyone. After I summarize the will, I'll outline the next steps, and you can ask any questions at that time."

Ian paused and papers rustled as everyone opened packets. The will was thick, and I quickly flipped through the pages. The back of the package contained an inventory with a total estimated value of the estate, over two hundred million dollars. When I'd combed through her files, I hadn't done the math. I had no idea she had that much money.

Ian began listing what Peg left each person. To her younger nephews and nieces, she left funds for college as well as enough money for a down payment on a house once they completed school. Of course, she left the business to Lou along with some money and some furniture in her townhome. Peg left Chantal with quite a bit of money contingent on her spending a year in rehab. I was sure that would go over big when she was sober enough to hear the news.

Peg left her townhome to Brad. Surprising. I thought she'd leave it to Chantal. Brad nudged my leg and pointed to the line in his copy of the will. I could tell he was also caught off guard. When Ian announced that Peg left her wine collection to Aunt

Jane, she glanced my way and winked. Toasts to Peg over a few glasses of wine were most likely in the future.

Peg left the foundation to Jenny along with several million dollars. There was a long list of who would receive the jewelry. She left several pieces to Karen, and I was touched that she left me a diamond and sapphire necklace, bracelet, and earring set. Tears started flowing down my face and onto the papers. Brad grabbed my hand and squeezed it, which of course did not go unnoticed by Jenny, who bumped me gently with her shoulder.

I remembered the gala when Peg wore the necklace, and I'd admired it. The event had benefitted Charleston's Arts and was a magical night filled with musical performances from various local artists and lots of dancing. Peg wore a sapphire-colored evening gown. She'd commented that the necklace would go great with my silver sequined cocktail dress and let me try it on. I told her it made me feel like a princess. She laughed and told me I was a princess and a high maintenance one.

The mention of my name brought me back to the present. Peg left me a piece of property in California, estimated value twenty million dollars, along with another million dollars in cash. I remembered seeing that property in the files. Flabbergasted, I wanted to jump out of my seat. What would I do with a piece of property on the other side of the country? Her note burned in my lap. I couldn't wait to read her explanation.

After forty-five minutes, Ian finally finished. "All the assets are either in a living trust or go directly to the beneficiary so there will be no probate court. As soon as I receive the death certificate, I'll provide each of you with copies. I've set up a separate email account to handle the disposition of the estate. Please use it for any correspondence. Irene and I will be communicating dates and timing for the next steps, so please ensure we have a good email address for you on the list in front. Any questions?"

I needed air. I almost toppled over my chair heading out. In no time, I flew out the back door and around to the side yard where I leaned against the wall and started sobbing. As much as I wanted to, I couldn't bear to open the letter. It would have to wait until I was home with the comfort of Duke by my side.

Instantly, Brad arrived beside me. He reached out and drew me into a bear hug. I cried against his chest until the tears stopped flowing. He pulled some Kleenex out of his pocket and handed it to me.

"Thanks. I must look a mess. I'm glad I wore my waterproof mascara."

"That was all a bit overwhelming wasn't it?"

"Yeah. I can't get my head around it. Much less my heart. The whole letter thing. Did you know about that?"

"No idea. Ian kept that to himself. It's pretty crazy. I may wait to read mine when I return to California." He wiped a stray tear off my cheek. "I better get back and help Ian. Are you OK?"

"I'll be fine. Thanks for allowing me to cry on your shoulder."

Brad cupped my chin to lift my face. "I'm here for you Liz, anytime." He gazed into my eyes for several moments before releasing his hand. "Can I take you to dinner tomorrow night?"

"I'd love to, but I can't. I'm headed to Paris to meet with Bjorn. When do you go back to California?"

"I'm leaving on Thursday. I'll call you. I know you are a big girl, but please be careful."

We walked back inside hand in hand. Jenny was deep in conversation with her dad. I retrieved my purse and quickly said my goodbyes. I couldn't wait to read Peg's letter.

Chapter 20

T he letter and the packet with the will were glaring at me from the kitchen counter. Pack first I told myself. Otherwise, it might not happen.

Pulling my suitcase down from the top shelf of the closet, I placed it on the bed and started laying out outfits. Duke plopped down on the rug beside me with a big sigh. He hated when I went out of town. Although he liked being boarded, he missed our routine and me. Counting the number of tops, pants, skirts, and dresses and reviewing my shoe selections, I concluded that I was well prepared for the trip. I placed my overflowing suitcase on the floor, leaving it open so I could add my cosmetic bag in the morning.

Probably over-packed. Oh, well.

For dinner, I threw together a fresh salad with some leftover chicken, placing a few chunks of chicken in Duke's bowl. After pouring a glass of chardonnay, Southern-style, in a Bell jar, I settled down at the kitchen table to eat. Exhausted, I was glad my flight didn't leave until later tomorrow. I wanted to read Peg's letter, but I just wasn't ready yet. What on earth was I supposed to do with a piece of land on the opposite coast? Overwhelmed by the thought of owning property in California, I needed time to let the news settle in.

While washing the dishes, I decided I would wait to read the letter in Paris. Peg would love that I read her note in one of her favorite places. Grabbing the documents, and my jar of chardonnay, I headed upstairs to my office. I packed the letter and the packet into the side pocket of my computer bag and gathered up my electronics, notebook, and European chargers.

Placing the computer bag next to my suitcase, I prepared for bed, praying for a good night's sleep. As soon as I changed into my pajamas, my phone buzzed. The police station. Again.

Sam's voice bellowed from the other end, "We need you to come down to the station tomorrow morning. Eight o'clock sharp."

"I have an appointment. Can't it wait?" Duke yipped from the other side of the room.

"Reschedule."

He hung up before I could respond. I couldn't imagine what was so urgent. I did the math. If I dropped Duke off at seven, I could be there by eight. My plane left at noon, so I should be able to make the flight.

The next morning, I dropped Duke off at the vet, tail wagging, happy to be doted on by a team of people who adored him. Arriving at the police station five minutes early, I was furious when Sam made me wait another ten minutes. A young male cop, who looked about ten, finally fetched me and walked me to the conference room where Sam and Matt were waiting. Matt stood as I walked into the room. Sam remained planted in his chair.

"Good morning." I nodded toward each of them. "So, what's this about?"

"How much did you know about Peg's will before yesterday?" Sam patted the copy of the will in front of him.

"I was completely shocked." I did know a little, but the bits that I knew were completely irrelevant.

Crossing his arms against his chest, Sam continued, "Method and motive, not looking too good for you Liz." The man had the audacity to grin. "Sure would like to see the letter she left you."

Suddenly it was too much. I couldn't stop the tears streaming down my face. "I haven't even read it yet. After I do, I'll give you a copy."

Matt slid a box of tissues my way and I mouthed a silent thank you.

"Ah, here we go. Lightweight Liz can't take a few questions from the cops. I have a hard time believing you ain't read that letter."

I glared at him for a full minute. Matt grew uncomfortable and said, "Sam, maybe we should wrap this up. Do you have any more questions for Liz?"

Sam drummed his fingers on the table. "Whatcha gonna do with all that money?"

I rolled my eyes toward the heavens. Lord, please. "I have no clue. I'm furious with Peg for leaving it to me and never mentioning a word about her intentions. It's one of the reasons I haven't read the letter yet."

"And the other reasons?" Sam asked.

"My business. Are we done here?" I turned toward Matt.

Matt glanced at Sam.

Sam replied. "For now. Just make yourself handy in case I have more questions."

It was not going to look good that I was headed halfway across the world.

***

I made my flight with ten minutes to spare. Walking onto the plane, I noticed Lou seated in the aisle seat in the same row as me.

"What a surprise." I air-kissed each of his cheeks and slid my carry-on into the overhead bin.

"Lizzie. Are you headed to Philly?

"No Paris," I stepped over him and slid into the window seat.

"Me too. What a fantastic coincidence."

I remembered the Post-It reminder to book a flight that I'd discovered while searching Lou's place. But really? The timing seemed like more than a coincidence. "What did you think about yesterday?" I asked, changing the subject.

"Emotional. I read my letter from Peg last night when I got home. I'm going to miss her so much." Lou choked on the words and wiped his eyes with his sleeve.

"I haven't read mine yet. I'm not ready." I stowed my computer bag underneath the seat in front of me and buckled my seat belt.

"What'll you do with the property in Cali?"

"No clue. I'm still surprised that she left that to me and never told me. I've turned it over and over in my head. Why?"

"You didn't know she was giving you that piece of land?" Lou seemed bewildered.

"No. Did you?"

"Umm, yeah." He hesitated and then continued. "I pulled her will out of the files before you got to the office. I needed to know what was happening with the business before I started calling clients."

Well, that explained the missing will. I decided to tell him the purpose of my visit upfront, so we didn't spend a long plane ride with the unspoken sitting between the two of us. "You might as well know…I'm headed to Paris to meet Bjorn. I need to know who this guy is."

The flight attendant interrupted our conversation with an offer of champagne. She winked at Lou. I grinned. Lots of luck with that one girl. We each took a flute and settled in to listen to her safety speech. Afterward, I put my headphones on as a clear signal that I didn't want to talk. A lot of good that did.

As soon as we were airborne, Lou tapped my shoulder. Perhaps when we changed planes in Philadelphia, I could switch my seat. I had a sinking feeling he was booked next to me the whole way.

"Liz, I have to confess, I saw your itinerary on your countertop. I thought that was probably what you were up to. I do have business in Paris, but I also didn't want you going alone. There are a few things I haven't told you about Bjorn."

Honestly, he couldn't tell me this in Charleston? I tapped my fingers on the armrest. I needed another drink. I wondered how quickly the flight attendant would be up and about with more cocktails. I removed my headphones and prepared to listen.

"There are rumors that Bjorn has Corsican mafia connections. You need to be careful. All our purchases were paid via wire into a Swiss bank account. Something always seemed off about that."

"You have to know by now that I can hold my own, although I appreciate you watching out for me. I saw you paid him via wire when I was sorting through the files."

"Yeah, I remember you asking me about that. Listen, Bjorn is charming and he cared for Peg, but I never trusted him." Shaking his head, he rubbed the back of his neck.

The flight attendant interrupted with an offer of a bowl of warm nuts and asked for our cocktail orders. Although I had work to do, I longed to curl up with an escape novel. I'd picked up a few promising reads from Blue Bicycle, my favorite bookshop, on my way to meet Jenny yesterday.

But work first.

As soon as the pilot gave the OK, I pulled out my laptop and researched the Corsican mafia. Hmm, interesting, also known as Le Milieu, they were violent and suspected of money laundering. Lou was right. I needed to proceed carefully. Maybe it wasn't so bad he'd decided to tag along.

On the second leg of our long flight over, I mapped out a reasonable and safe plan. I was all set to meet with Bjorn two days after I arrived in Paris. I wanted some time to emerge from jet-lag fog. Reviewing my notes, I sent an email to Liam to give him a quick update and let him know I'd be in Paris for a couple of days. Satisfied, I closed my laptop. I slipped off my shoes, pulled on the plane-provided socks, and settled in to read Laura Child's *Sweet Tea Revenge*. I sipped on the cabernet that was paired with the beef tenderloin filet I selected for dinner. Not long after dessert, I drifted into a restless sleep. Lou softly snored next to me.

Eight hours later, we arrived at Charles de Gaulle airport. After retrieving our luggage, we caught the first available taxi. I was grateful that Lou spoke fluent French. He easily conversed with the driver. Tired from the trip, I stared out the window. Paris brought back a flood of memories. My last visit had been my honeymoon.

Full of hope, Sawyer had said the night lights of Paris twinkled in my eyes. We'd just graduated from college and had jobs waiting for us in Atlanta. We were looking forward to house shopping. The air had pulsed with possibilities. We spent ten blissful days in Paris. Exploring, eating, drinking, making love.

The marriage lasted six years. We both wanted a family. We tried so hard to conceive, eventually resorting to endless fertility treatments. I'd been ecstatic when I finally became pregnant. Six months into my pregnancy, my doctor told me our baby girl had died in utero. Another doctor's appointment that I'd attended alone. We were both devastated. I cried nonstop for weeks. Sawyer buried himself in his work. When I discovered later that Sawyer had cheated on me, we were done.

My thoughts were interrupted when the taxi driver pulled up in front of the hotel. Yes, of course, Lou was staying here too.

Formally-dressed bellhops took our names and whisked our luggage away. Peg used to rave about the Keppler Hotel. As we stepped inside to register, I could see why. The black and white lobby was peppered with animal print accents. Orchid plants in vivid hues of purple and pink, as well as other small pops of color accented black lacquer tables. Tall, black metal statues of dogs guarded a fireplace in a cozy corner. Tufted black and white striped chairs formed a half-circle in front of the fireplace. Light poured through a glass dome ceiling framed with a beautiful crown molding. The musical sound of the French language hummed through the space.

After retrieving our room keys, Lou took my hand and pulled me into the dining room. "You have to see the restaurant, Liz." The space was taupe with black accents. Vases filled with white carnations and greenery commanded the center on each table. One wall was covered in magnolia wallpaper and the seats and backs of the chairs were covered in matching magnolia fabric. We could be in Charleston. "Did you guys decorate this place?"

"Not the whole place. But we did redo this dining room a few months ago. Don't you just love it?"

"It's amazing. What do you say we grab a quick bite and then call it a night?"

After supper, Lou and I agreed to meet up for breakfast in the morning. Exhausted, I just wanted to crawl into my fluffy queen-sized bed and fall into a dreamless sleep. Peg's letter burned in the side pocket of my computer bag waiting to be read.

But it would have to wait.

Chapter 21

The next morning, I rolled out of bed and glanced at my phone. Ten o'clock. Three missed calls from Lou. I checked my voicemail. His last message said to please call him as soon as I could. Feeling guilty, I phoned him back. If I was Duke, my tail would be tucked between my legs.

"Lou, I'm so sorry. I slept right through. I'm shocked that I slept so soundly."

"It's OK. I'm just about finished, and breakfast ends at ten-thirty. Do you want anything? A croissant? A cup of tea?"

This morning I didn't want a cup of tea. I wanted a nice strong cup of coffee. "Oh my god, you're a saint. I'd love a croissant. And forget the tea. I need coffee today."

"Cream? Sugar?" he asked.

"Yes and yes and thank you." Slipping into the hotel provided robe, I thumbed through messages on my phone as I waited Lou's arrival.

He knocked at my door ten minutes later. "Room service."

I opened the door and grabbed the coffee out of his hand. "Lou, you're my hero. Come in. What do you have planned for today?" He looked very Parisian, dressed in gray pants and a navy long-sleeved shirt. Sunglasses were perched on top of his wavy black hair.

"I need to check on a couple of orders, and I plan on scoping out a few antique stores. Plus, I need to meet with a client who saw our work and wants to hire us to redo her restaurant." He caught himself and said, "I guess I mean hire me. She doesn't know about Peg yet. I want to tell her in person. What about you? What are you up to?"

I filled him in on my plan to visit the museums and take the day off to rest.

"Liz, promise me you'll be careful."

"I promise." I crossed my heart for emphasis. "No PI today. Today just jet-lagged Liz recovering."

We agreed to meet for cocktails in the hotel bar at six o'clock that evening.

Lou couldn't resist one more emphatic "Remember. You promised." He pointed his index finger at me as he closed the door to my room.

***

Oh my, I loved Monet, and what an intimate setting. The Louvre and Musée d' Orsay were incredible. However, they didn't hold a candle to Musée de l'Orangerie. I found a spot on a bench in front of Monet's Water Lilies and pulled out Peg's letter. The first part was typed and generic and addressed to "My dear family and friends." I assumed everyone's letter contained these paragraphs. The last part was handwritten and addressed specifically to me.

My Dear Family and Friends,

If you are reading this, it means I'm gone too soon. Please know I've had an amazing life with few regrets. A life enriched by each and every one of you. How lucky was I to be surrounded by so much love? Please also know I believe in God and Jesus Christ, and I do believe there is an afterlife. I hope some of you will find peace and comfort in that. Some of you will be surprised at the wealth I amassed. I was very fortunate with the money I inherited, and I made some decent investments. I put a lot of thought into what I left each of you. Please don't bicker and quarrel. My choices were made with love, please respect that. I put my affairs in good hands with Ian and Irene. Please make it easy on them. May God bless each of you.

Much love,

Peg

Dear Liz,

What a blessing you have been! That day in the park was fate–and then to find out you lived just a few houses away. We've only known each other a handful of years, but it feels like I've known you all my life. Your friendship means so much to me. It was so refreshing to have a friend who didn't know Alex and me as a couple.

I've always admired your strength, courage, and style. You are a beautiful person inside and out. Please don't be upset that I didn't tell you how much money I had. I just didn't like to talk about it.

Please look after Jenny. She needs a "big sis" in her life. I know it will be hard for her when I'm gone. I have a big favor to ask–will you help with the audits of the charities for the foundation? It's right up your alley. You'll do a fantastic job of it and hopefully the money I left you will help with any financial burden.

About that … There's another person I'm worried about, Brad. He works too much … maybe you could spend some time with him when you are in California deciding what to do about the piece of property? He's a terrific guy, and I regret that the three of us didn't do more together when he was in town so you would know him better. I guess I didn't want to share my two best friends.

One last favor—will you keep an eye out for Tina?

We had some fun times and many laughs, didn't we? And a few good cries too. I'll miss you. I'm applying for the job of your Guardian Angel, I know it will be a full-time one!

If you see a hummingbird, think of me. You know they are my favorite.

Love you forever,

Peg

Tears streamed down my face. I remembered that fateful day in the park when we'd first met.

Peg had been sitting on the fountain's ledge, resting after a hard run. Duke, spotting another spot to swim and play, lunged forward jerking his leash from my hand. He ran straight toward Peg and leaped into the water, spraying murky water all over her white running pants and matching white racer top. I stood paralyzed, my mouth in a big 'O,' each movement playing in slow motion. Peg leaped up and jumped into the water, toppling over while trying to grab Duke's leash. She emerged soaked, Duke trailing behind her. "Is this your puppy?" she said, her long black ponytail dripping. I looked at them both and doubled over in laughter. Peg looked at herself and joined me, both of us giggling like ten-year-olds. When we exchanged contact information, we discovered that I was the new neighbor in her townhome community.

Brought back to the present by a hand on my shoulder, I looked up and saw an older woman who rattled some words off in French. I assumed she asked if I was OK. While nodding, I said one of the few words I knew, "Bien." Patting my shoulder, she went on her way. I placed Peg's letter back in my bag, pulled out some Kleenex, and attempted to regain my composure.

After completing the tour of the museum, my heart felt somewhat less heavy. The colors and textures of Monet's paintings brought me some measure of peace. Although my emotions were still raw, it was time to move on to some recon work. OK, I know I promised, but it couldn't be helped. I had a murder to solve. Anyway, I did have my fingers crossed on the hand behind my back when I vowed to rest today. No need to tell Lou about this little side trip after my visit to Musée de l'Orangerie. The more I knew about Bjorn before our meeting tomorrow, the better I'd feel.

La Maison de Bjorn was just around the corner from the museum. The store was part of a long two-story pale pink building. Black cursive lettering over the door identified the name of the business. The front door was constructed of heavy wood, a black iron lion's head knocker rested in the center. I wondered if you had to ring the doorbell to get in. Boxes filled with fuchsia and orange geraniums were underneath windows framed by black shutters. I kept my distance, taking a seat on a bench on the other side of the street to observe for a moment. My feet needed the rest.

I pulled my notepad out of my tote and started sketching. I used the left side of my brain so much, it helped to engage the right side. Lighted crystal chandeliers of various sizes and shapes sparkled from inside the store, inviting passers-by to window shop. One window showcased a beautiful cherry buffet, topped with silver candelabras and blue and white Wedgewood vases filled with peach-colored roses. I admired the décor. It was enough to catch the eye and invite a view deeper into the store. The next window had a small lady's Chippendale style curved desk. Behind the desk was a Chippendale chair covered in teal fabric. On top of the desk were antique books wedged between iron bookends. A large brass floor lamp completed the ensemble. A florist and a patisserie anchored the shop on either side.

I remembered Peg mentioning a bakery nearby that had the most incredible chocolate éclairs. She said it was almost as good as our favorite in Charleston, Sugar Bakeshop. Placing my notepad back in my tote, I decided to go check it out.

The shop was small, and the odor of freshly baked pastries filled the air. I had a feeling the smell would linger on my clothes for a while. Not that I minded. The aroma was amazing. I lingered over all of the yummy choices in the glass case. Apricot and lemon tarts, a cherry parfait, an apple pie, a cheesy crepe, various croissants and then the éclairs. Ooh, la la.

The woman at the counter was in her late fifties, with white wiry hair pulled back in a ponytail. She was not as overweight as I'd be if I worked here. Her sapphire-colored eyes seemed friendly. I must have had American written all over me because she asked, "How can I help you?" in heavily accented English. Maybe it had been pulling up the translation app on my phone that had tipped her off.

I took a chance and said, "My friend, Peg, raves about your chocolate éclairs. I'll take one of those."

"Ah, the lovely Peg. So, you from South Carolina too?" she asked.

"Yes." Do I tell her or not tell her? I didn't want her tipping off Bjorn. I decided not. "I'm here visiting with a friend. I just had to come to try the éclairs."

"Excellente. So? You also know Bjorn next door?"

I hadn't anticipated that question. I quickly concocted a reply. "No, I've never met him, but Peg talked about him all the time. How long have you known Bjorn?"

"I open café ten or so years ago. He had shop with wife, Nicole, then. She work a couple days a week. We make friends. Still friends after divorce. Bjorn not happy about that. Maybe, you know, with divorce usually remain with one side or other?" She asked in broken English.

I nodded. "You're the owner?"

"Oui."

I handed her my credit card and paid. Threading through the tables, I made my way to a small painted wrought iron table with two café chairs and sank my teeth into the éclair. The pastry was soft and flaky, and the chocolate topping was creamy with a hint of coffee and caramel. The vanilla cream oozed out the sides. I caught a drop with my tongue, savoring the flavors.

The shop owner walked my way with a steaming cup of coffee laced with frothed milk.

"Latté, how you say? On the house. You must try flavors together."

"Thank you. This is delicious," I said.

"Merci. Friend of Peg also friend of me. You two are close?"

"Very," I replied.

"Ah, you must be Liz. Peg so wanted to bring you here. She tell me, my best friend, Liz. She would love this place."

The moment she said that Peg wanted to bring me here, my eyes teared, and I dabbed at the corners with a napkin.

"So sorry. Not meant to make you cry." She reached out and patted my arm.

"What's your name?" I asked.

She held out her hand. "Annalise. Pleased to meet you, Liz."

She hesitated a moment and then said, "Listen. I feel I must say my thoughts. Peg and Bjorn. They are good together. But … he has problems. I try tell Peg. She only sees good."

"What kind of difficulties?" I asked.

"Money. Too much lost in divorce. Many strange men going in and out of his shop. Sometimes they come here. I no like them. Not good over there." She waved a hand toward Bjorn's shop. "I worry, so does his ex."

She started back to the counter, then turned. "Why Peg not come with you?"

The cafe had emptied, and I decided to tell her. After all, she was being open with me. "Annalise, I'm sorry to be the bearer of bad news, but Peg passed away about two weeks ago."

Annalise's hands flew to her heart, and her skin turned a shade paler. She plopped into the chair next to me. "Merde. No. Passed away, you mean she gone? Dead? How?"

"She was murdered. Shot. I'm actually here investigating. I'm meeting Bjorn tomorrow. I want to ask him some questions."

Tears ran in streams down Annalise's cheeks, and she swiped at them in an effort to compose herself. "That pig. You think he tell me? No? He gone last week. But he could call, no?" She stood up. "Peg tell me you are investigator. I give you something."

Returning from the back of the shop, she handed me a piece of paper and her business card. "Man from DGSE come in. Maybe three week ago. He ask questions about Bjorn. I give you copy of card. You contact him. Tell him, Annalise give you. Plez, you must let me know what happens."

I happened to know the DGSE was the French equivalent of the CIA. I handed her one of my cards. "Yes, please. Let's stay in touch. Do me a favor, if you see Bjorn don't tell him I was here today. I don't want him to know I'm snooping."

"Snooping mean spying?"

I nodded.

"Ah yes, of course. I no tell. But I throw pie at him for not telling me about Peg. Be careful, ma chérie."

Chapter 22

On the cab ride back to the hotel, I punched in the number Annalise had given me for Jean-Paul Claudette, senior detective. I expected to get voicemail, instead, a raspy voice answered.

"J.P., allô?"

"Parlez vous Anglais?"

"Yes. Who is this?"

He sounded like a man in a hurry, so I quickly filled him in on why I was calling and how I came across his name. "Any chance you can meet me while I'm in town?"

"Yes. Where are you staying? When do you meet Bjorn?"

"I have an appointment tomorrow at two o'clock. Staying at the Keppler," I replied.

"Are you free tonight?"

"Yes, what time?"

"Let's meet in the bar at the Keppler at six."

"What do you look like?" I asked.

"I'll find you. I know what you look like. I've been paying a bit of attention to what happened in Charleston. *Á bientôt.*"

As soon as I arrived back at the hotel, I phoned Lou's room.

"Liz, I was just about to call you. Jet lag hit me hard this trip. Do you mind if we skip tonight? I'm ordering room service and calling it an early night."

"That works. Breakfast in the morning, 9ish?"

"Sure, doll. See you then."

"Sweet dreams. Hope you sleep well."

Relieved that I didn't have to make up an excuse for postponing our original plans, I filled the tub with hot water and poured in the hotel-provided lavender-scented bubble bath. I had just enough time to take a bath and freshen up before meeting Jean-Paul. I slipped on a simple black sheath dress that traveled well and a pair of black flats. My feet were tired after walking most of the day. Adding a gold necklace and earrings, I checked my appearance in the full-length mirror one more time before heading downstairs. Other than the dark circles under my eyes, not bad.

At about five minutes past six, I walked into the bar, scanning the room for J.P.

A man in a navy sports coat, white oxford shirt, and gray pants rose from a table on the left and waved my way. As I approached, I saw that he was quite handsome in a rugged kind of way. Early forties, jet-black hair with hints of gray, skin tanned and lined. Bushy eyebrows framed dreamy heavily lashed amber-colored eyes. Not my usual type, but that kiss from Brad had awakened my libido and since then I'd started noticing every halfway decent-looking guy. J.P. was definitely more than halfway.

Reaching out his right hand, he said, "Ah Liz, you look lovely." I extended my hand expecting a firm handshake. Instead, he bent down and placed a light kiss on my hand. The stubble from his five o'clock shadow tickled.

Pulling out a chair for me, he said, "I hope you don't think I'm too assuming. I ordered a nice bottle of a French Bordeaux." He sat across from me and poured each of us a glass. "I think you will like it." I was enchanted by the musical tones in his accent. Soothing, like listening to soft instrumental jazz.

After swirling the red liquid and inhaling the complex aromas of leather, coffee, and spices, I took a sip. "Hmm, this is fantastic." The wine was smooth with a lingering after-taste.

"One of my favorites. When in France," He held his wine glass up, "Salut."

"Cheers." We clinked glasses. With the formalities out of the way, we quickly got down to business.

"You said you were following what was happening in Charleston? Why?" I couldn't imagine why the DGSE would be interested in Peg's murder.

He shrugged, "We've been watching Bjorn closely, including anyone he's involved with."

"Do you think he had anything to do with Peg's death?"

He deflected the question. "Tell me what you know about Bjorn."

I filled him in on the little I knew about the man. J.P. listened, interrupting occasionally with a clarifying question.

"You must tread carefully Liz. Your friend, Lou, is correct. Bjorn does associate with the Corsican mafia, and we believe they are using him to launder money through his antique business. So far, we haven't been able to prove it."

"Wait." I dug into my tote, pulled out my notebook, and flipped to the notes I'd made while perusing through Peg's files. "I took pictures of a few invoices. The payment arrangement seemed strange." I pulled the pictures up on my phone and showed them to JP.

Placing his hand over mine, he said, "Merci, Liz. This is most helpful. Will you forward those to me?" His hands were large and calloused, his fingernails well-manicured. For a moment, I imagined those hands on my body. I quickly withdrew my hand and he poured each of us a second glass of wine.

After I confirmed his contact information, the conversation switched to our professions. "I see you take copious notes. Mine are quite cryptic." He whipped out a small leather notebook from his right inside coat pocket and tucked the paper with the address and contact information inside. I noticed that he carried. A small weapon was well hidden underneath the jacket.

"You'll laugh," I said reaching inside my purse and pulling out my stack of index cards.

"A woman after my own heart. I do the same," he said with a smile.

We shared different tips and techniques. The waiter interrupted, asking if we would like another bottle of wine. J.P. asked him to give us a minute.

"Liz, I would like to take you to dinner and continue our conversation. A proper French dinner. There's a fabulous restaurant around the corner you must experience. A Paris visit isn't complete without it."

"I'd love that." My stomach grumbled reminding me that I hadn't had anything to eat since the earlier éclair.

The restaurant was small, maybe thirty tables, each covered in a white linen tablecloth. The wait staff were dressed in tuxedos. The lighting from the chandeliers was dim and candles glowed in crystal glasses. A vase with a single red rose sat in the center of each table. Fancy and romantic. J.P. gave his name to the hostess and gave me a wink.

We walked across the glowing white and khaki-checkered tile floors to our table. The chairs were Louis XIV style and covered in gold and white-striped fabric. J.P. insisted on pulling out my chair and then ordered another bottle of the same wine we'd had at the hotel. He definitely could be a bit presumptuous. But right now, I was enjoying someone else making the decisions.

When I opened the menu, J.P. put a hand on my arm. "Liz, please, you must let me order for you. Trust me."

Our waiter returned with the wine, and J.P. placed our order. I noticed the waiter didn't write anything down. I've always admired people who could do that.

"Tell me about the case," he said.

Ugh. I so didn't want to go there, but I'd come to respect his professionalism in the short time we'd been together. Maybe he would catch a clue I had missed.

The waiter arrived with our first course. Caviar on rounds of toasted garlic bread topped with a creamy sauce and lightly garnished with chives. Even though I wasn't a fan of caviar, I had to admire the presentation.

Postponing taking a bite, I filled him in on the work I'd done so far. I pulled my notebook out of my bag and flipped through it to ensure that I didn't leave any major points out. I chose not to go into greater detail. Otherwise, we would be here all night.

He listened intently.

"What do you think?" I asked when I finished.

"I think you should eat your caviar," he replied.

Not wanting to be impolite, I took a bite. The flavors exploded inside my mouth. For a moment I closed my eyes and inhaled the smells. I took another bite. The cream sauce was tart, a perfect dressing for the smoky caviar, the textures offset by the crunchiness of the garlic toast. Amazing how the flavors seemed to layer over each other. "Wow," I said.

"I told you. You can trust me." He smiled. "So, here are my thoughts. First, you are doing an amazing and thorough job at breakneck speed in a situation that must be very trying for you."

I blushed at the compliment. "Thank you."

"I know the police in the States consider you a prime suspect, but I do not. And I have good instincts. If I thought you had murdered your friend I wouldn't have agreed to meet with you." He took a sip of his wine. "I do think there are areas you need to explore more deeply, the connection to Bjorn being one of them. And you are glossing over Lou. I'm not saying he did it, but he lives in the neighborhood, and they were business partners. He is a viable suspect."

We were both quiet for a few minutes, eating and sipping our wine as he let the advice sink in.

"You're right," I admitted. "I guess I just can't stand the possibility. If he did it, then I will lose another dear friend." My eyes misted, and I was grateful for the arrival of the waiter with our second course.

My mood quickly lifted as he placed the gold-rimmed china plates in front of us. A lobster tail accompanied by a rainbow of fresh vegetables. Lobster was my favorite food on the planet.

"Bon appétit." We clinked glasses.

"Is there anything else you want to know J.P.?"

"Non, ma chérie. Let's enjoy each other's company for a spell. Tell me about yourself."

"No, no. You first. I've been doing all the talking. Plus, I want to enjoy the lobster." Dipping a forkful into garlic butter, I savored the sweet tender meat. Sighing with pure contentment, I asked, "How did you end up working for DGSE?"

"My family has been in law enforcement for generations. I never seriously considered another career. Not only is it a decent living, but the sense of service and satisfaction of bringing a situation to justice can't be duplicated for me. At one time, I thought about becoming a barrister." He shrugged. "Now, just the occasional testimony is enough of a courtroom visit for me."

At his insistence, I filled J.P. in on my corporate career and eventual move to Charleston to become a PI, conveniently leaving out the marriage and divorce bit.

"Do you have a family?" I asked, "Wife, kids?"

He held up both his hands, devoid of any rings. "Married to the job I'm afraid. A few serious relationships here and there. This profession is tough on a relationship. It takes the right person. You?"

"Married once, it didn't work out. The kid thing didn't work out either. I do have a wonderful dog-kid though, Duke," I pulled out my phone and showed him a couple of pictures.

After dinner, J.P. insisted on walking me back to the hotel. I was pleasantly full and slightly tipsy. I didn't mind a bit when he held my hand, caressing my palm. A gentleman, he walked on the outside, protecting me from the street. He adjusted his stride to mine and we walked in silence. I could feel a slow heat building between us. Not electric, like what I experienced with Brad. This, I've felt before. Two people who were enjoying each other's company and may want to take the next step, no strings attached.

We walked into the lobby and I turned to him and said, "Come upstairs."

"Are you sure?" he asked.

"Yes," I replied without hesitation.

The intensity built on the short ride up the elevator. I fumbled with my room key and J.P. took it from me and easily swiped it.

Afterward, I expected him to leave. He surprised me by slipping underneath the covers and pulling me close.

Chapter 23

The next morning I awakened early to the buzzing of my phone. The bed was empty. An envelope with my name sat on top of the end table. It was only six o'clock. Ugh.

"Hello?" I answered with a yawn.

"Hi Liz, it's me, Brad. Were you asleep? You sound groggy."

"Just waking up." I sat up, dangling my legs over the side of the bed.

"Should I call back?"

"No, it's OK. I'm up." I took a long sip of water from the bottle of water on the nightstand. I didn't feel hung over. Must have been an excellent wine.

"Just wanted to check in with you and see how it's going."

Last night with J.P. was nice, but Brad's voice tugged at my heart and I was reminded of Peg's request in her note. I wanted to get to know him better. Glancing at the crumbled sheets, I felt immediately guilty for what was most likely a one-night stand.

For the next few minutes, we chatted about the case, Paris, and Brad's training for the upcoming Ironman in San Diego.

"I'm not sure when I'll make it back to Charleston. But I'd like to see you again. Would you consider coming to California?"

"Of course. I should check out that piece of property." The words tumbled out of my mouth without thought.

"Great. How 'bout the week of July 15th ? It's the week of Peg's birthday. Mine too. It'll be tough this year."

"Sounds good, but it depends upon the investigation. Let me get back to you." I prayed that I'd solve the mystery of her murder by then.

"Have you read your letter?" he asked.

"Yeah. Yesterday at the Musée de l'Orangerie. I thought Peg would approve of the setting. Although a public place may not have been the best for me. I couldn't stop crying."

"I read mine on the plane ride home. Glad it was just me, the pilot and stewardess on the plane. I was an emotional wreck."

Must be nice to travel private. For a moment, I was jealous at the thought of the stewardess comforting him.

"Peg asked me to stay in touch with you." He cleared his throat. "Get to know you better."

"She said the same to me about you," I replied.

"I won't mind that. Oh, and Liz, I bought it."

"Bought what?" I expected him to tell me about some fancy new bike or some other man toy.

"Amazing Grace. I missed the smell of you."

For the last eight months, my love life had been comatose. And it just shifted to the speed of light in the space of a week. I didn't know what to say.

Brad chuckled on the other end. "I can tell I've stunned you into silence. Good luck with Bjorn and please be careful. Call me after you meet him, OK? I don't care what time it is."

After the call ended, I heated some water in the hotel-provided teapot and fixed a cup of tea. I'd have preferred milk, but the small plastic containers of cream would do. Letting the tea steep, I reached for the envelope J.P. had left behind.

> Ma chérie Liz,
>
> Good morning. Thank you so much for last night. You are wonderful company, and I enjoyed our evening together. I had an emergency call during the night and had to leave. Please forgive me. You were sleeping quite soundly.
>
> Be careful with Bjorn, and please call me after you meet with him. I'd love to see you again before you leave.
>
> All the best,
>
> J.P.

Brad and I weren't exclusively dating but somehow I felt disloyal. Sighing, I tucked the note back in the envelope. I needed to bring the relationship with J.P. back to a professional level. This was starting to get complicated, and I didn't like complicated.

I looked at the time, two more hours before I'd meet Lou for breakfast. I needed to prepare for my meeting with Bjorn and catch up on email. I started with the latter, opening a note from Jenny.

> Hi Liz,
>
> I hope you're having a grand time in Paris. I remember when Aunt Peg took me there after high school graduation. We had a blast. I love that city.
>
> I discovered the big family secret! And boy is it interesting. Aunt Jane and I put the pieces together.
>
> I'm worried about Jackson. I think he might be back

on drugs. He's been missing since Friday. I have no idea where he is. I don't know what to do. Dad's torn up about it. Me too.

Call me when you get a chance. Stay safe.

Love you,

Jenny

I sent a quick response.

Hi Jenny,

Thanks so much for the note. Fantastic work! I can't wait to hear what you found out. Will you send me a recent picture of Jackson? Maybe I can circulate it and help find him.

And yes, Paris is amazing. I have plenty to tell you when I return. OK, if I call you later? Say 9:00 or so your time?

Love you, too,

Liz

After creating a list of questions to ask Bjorn, I hopped in the shower and then opened the small closet and contemplated what to wear. I finally selected a pastel floral blouse with ruffled sleeves paired with a skirt and some strappy sandals. Maybe the feminine approach would catch Bjorn off guard. Before I went downstairs to meet Lou, I placed a quick call to Gunner.

"Yo, Liz. How you doing?"

"OK. I have another favor to ask." I didn't mention I was half-way across the world. No reason for him to worry.

"Shoot," Gunner replied.

"Peg's nephew, Jackson, is missing. He has a drug problem. Do you mind checking around to see if anyone has seen him? I'd be especially interested if he was caught on any of the cameras the night of Peg's murder. I'll forward his picture to you."

"You think he had anything to do with the murder?"

"Not sure. Maybe. If he was there, maybe he saw something. It's a loose end, and you know how much I like those," I said.

"Did a good job of teaching you. You got it. Send me the pic, and I'll see what I can find out."

***

"You look lovely and well-rested." Lou let out a slight whistle.

"Thanks. You look like you had a good night's sleep, too." I settled into the dining room chair and checked out the breakfast menu.

"Listen, Liz. I'm going with you when you meet Bjorn. No arguing."

"No way. It'll throw off the whole dynamic." What was it with all these men suddenly all protective of me? "I'm a big girl. I have this."

"I know Bjorn. Maybe I can help. I don't like you meeting with him alone. What if he's the murderer? What if he thinks you're getting too close? I couldn't stand it if something happened to you, especially with me right here."

My hackles were up, but I quickly calmed down with that comment. We had both been through the emotional wringer. "Tell you what. How bout I have your number up on my phone? Ready to call if I feel threatened. If you get a call from me, you'll know to come in. You can camp at the pastry shop next door."

"How do you know about the pastry shop?" Lou asked.

Yikes, almost busted. "Peg used to rave about it."

Lou looked at me like he didn't believe me, and I thought I really was busted. Then he relaxed. "I still don't like you going alone, but I guess that'll work. What are you doing this morning?"

"I'd like to squeeze in a little shopping. You?"

"I have a few more people to catch up with. Let's meet up for lunch, and we can head Bjorn's way together."

***

Bjorn stood waiting by the door when I walked in. "Ah, you must be Liz. So pleased to meet you. I wish it was under better circumstances." Bjorn reached for my hand and kissed the top of it. "You look just like Peg described, although I imagined you a little taller."

Bjorn towered over me. Broad-shouldered, he was likely at least 6'3," not the typical Frenchman. His mahogany hair was curly and a little on the longish side. Dressed impeccably in a white starched shirt with monogrammed cufflinks, he wore dark gray pants that appeared to be freshly pressed. His black leather belt and shoes probably cost a fortune. He and Peg must have made a handsome couple.

"Come. Let's go sit in my office." I followed him as he turned to an assistant and said, "Sofia, please no interruptions unless absolutely necessary."

A large ornate antique cherry-wood desk stood in the center of Bjorn's office. The walls were beige and adorned with oil paintings of the French countryside. A beautiful oriental rug in shades of brown and red covered most of the wood floor. A slight scent of cigar smoke hung in the room. Bjorn pulled out one of the two burgundy leather chairs in front of the desk and motioned for me to sit.

"Please have a seat. Can I get you a drink?"

"No thank you."

I commented on his perfect English.

"Thank you, I lived in New York City for a while." Settling into the large burgundy leather chair behind the desk, he said, "I'm sure you didn't travel all this way just to meet me. Peg told me what you do for a living. If you're investigating her murder, I don't know if I can help. I can't imagine anyone wanting to hurt Peg."

His words stung. Peg and Bjorn talked about me, yet she never mentioned Bjorn to me. "I have just a few questions for you if you don't mind."

"Go ahead."

"Tell me about your business. How long have you been here?"

"I opened the shop almost twenty years ago. I tend to cater to an upscale clientele. My pieces are from all over the world. Antiquing runs in the family. My uncle owns a shop in the South of France. I loved spending time there as a kid. I was delighted when Peg and Lou discovered the shop. I remember the first time she walked through the doors." His emerald eyes, framed by long black lashes misted up with the memory.

"She was wearing a white linen shirt with a short black skirt that highlighted her incredible legs. Even the jewelry I remember, heavy gold chain, gold bangles, and gold hoop earrings. She looked so Parisian, her long dark hair tumbling down her shoulders. Forgive me." Bjorn opened a drawer and pulled out a monogrammed handkerchief. He wiped away the tears that were rolling down his cheeks.

Composing himself, he continued. He seemed like the type of person who liked to hear himself talk. "She and Lou were admiring an armoire. I walked up and introduced myself. I couldn't stop staring at her. She was so beautiful."

I noticed he had no problem speaking about her in the past tense. I found that a bit troubling. Although, most of us were still slipping back and forth as we adjusted to the idea that she was gone from our lives.

"I managed to convince her to extend her stay and come with me to the South of France to see some of my uncle's pieces. Lou returned to Charleston to tend the shop. And, well, I'm sure you know the rest of the story."

"It'd be nice to hear it from you." I closely observed his body language as he continued the story of their relationship. His arms were perched on either side of the desk. Leaning forward only occasionally, he glanced away from me as he reminisced, recalling details of their times together. I found myself comforted that Peg did have some great times during those last few months of her life.

"I need to ask you some tougher questions." I paused for effect. "Where were you the night Peg died?"

"It's an easy question. On a plane to South Africa to attend an antique conference in Cape Town. I learned of her death two days later from Lou. I couldn't believe it. I still can't believe it."

"Why didn't you attend the service?" I asked.

Bjorn pushed away from the desk slightly and leaned back in his chair. He started to fidget with a Mont Blanc pen.

"The flight would have cost me a lot since it was such short notice, and I was fresh out of miles. I'd given them to my ex and our daughters for a summer trip."

Interesting. Perhaps there was some truth to the speculation of money troubles. "Tell me about your business dealings with PeggyLou."

"Honestly, they were one of the easiest teams I've worked with. Mostly I dealt with Peg. But all dealings were fairly seamless. I could contact either one of them about a piece they might like, or a piece they were looking for. We'd FaceTime. Or if the time difference made it impossible, I'd send pictures. I appreciated that one partner could make a decision without consulting the other. I was able to move faster, and it cut the risk of them losing the piece in the interim."

"I noticed the invoices were from CM Partners Ltd.?"

"Yes. It's my uncle's company. I'm a partner."

"Why a Swiss bank account"

"Oh, that." Bjorn glanced down, avoiding eye contact. "It's pretty simple. We—"

Bjorn's assistant and an older short, stocky bald man burst into the office. "I'm so sorry for the interruption, Bjorn. Marcus insisted on talking to you." The other man's face was flushed, his hands clenched.

Bjorn abruptly stood. "Excuse me, Liz. I'll be right back."

The men walked out of the office, and I followed, veering off to the left where I saw a sign for the restroom. Marcus and Bjorn joined two other men in the far corner of the shop. Ducking out of their view, I peered around the corner and strained my ears to pick up the exchange. The voices grew louder but they were speaking in rapid French. I could only pick up an occasional word. Not enough to get the gist of the conversation. The shouting intensified, and one of the men slammed a notebook on a nearby table. A vase tumbled and crashed to the floor with a clatter. The men marched out the door leaving shards of the broken glass behind.

A minute later, Lou came racing through the front door. Bjorn's assistant grabbed Lou's arm and hustled us both back to Bjorn's office. The restroom would have to wait.

"Lou what are you doing here, I didn't call you."

"I didn't like the look of those men. Neither did Annalise. She's the one who insisted I come and rescue you. You could've told me you went to visit her the other day."

I shrugged. "Sorry."

Before Lou could respond, Bjorn reentered the office and embraced Lou. "Lou, I had no idea you were in town."

Despite Lou's dislike of Bjorn, he embraced him. Stepping back, he explained. "I came with Liz. I've been meaning to call you."

"How are you, Lou?"

"Hanging in there. You?"

"Taking it a day at a time. But we go on, yes?"

Lou nodded.

"While you're here, I have a few pieces we just received that I would like to show you. Liz, you don't mind, do you? We were finished, yes?"

"Actually, no. What just happened?"

"Just some confusion over some paperwork and some billing. They work for a company that I purchase some of my antiques from." Bjorn fidgeted with his cufflink.

"They seemed pretty upset."

"Short fuses. How about those pieces, Lou?"

"I'd love to see them."

I glared at Lou. "You two go ahead. Lou, I'll be at the patisserie waiting."

Outside, I found a quiet place to call J.P. He answered right away.

"Allô, Liz. How did it go?"

I told him about the meeting and described the men who'd interrupted us, including the one named Marcus. "I'm not crazy about Bjorn. He's a little shady, but he does have an alibi. And I do believe his emotions around Peg's death are genuine. He was somewhat vague when I asked him about CM Partners and the payment arrangements."

"I can't share much at this point but we're investigating them." He paused and then continued. "Have you come across anything indicating that Peg was concerned about Bjorn's suspicious business arrangements?"

"No."

"Do you still consider him a suspect?"

I thought for a moment. "I haven't decided."

"Unless he thought she was on to him, what would be his motive for killing her?" J.P. asked.

"There's always the classic motives. Money and jealousy? I'm not sure, but you've given me some paths to explore."

"I'm working tonight but are you free tomorrow night? I'd like to see you again."

"We head out around noon tomorrow. It's a short trip."

"Ah, well, lovely Liz. Until we meet again. Stay in touch and call if you need to discuss the case."

"Thanks, J.P. For everything."

"Avec plaisir. I will cherish the memory of your beautiful body."

So much for ending the conversation on a professional note.

Chapter 24

I walked toward the pastry shop while texting Brad. It was a little early in California, and I just wasn't ready to talk after the conversation with J.P. Annalise greeted me with a hug and shepherded me to a table already set with a chocolate éclair. "On the house. You must tell me about men next door."

"They had some kind of heated discussion with Bjorn. Didn't last long, and the French was too rapid for me to make out any of the conversation."

"I come back with coffee."

Annalise returned a few moments later with coffee for both of us. As soon as she sat in her chair, a group of students poured through the door.

She muttered as she left to wait on them. I sipped my coffee and then took a bite of éclair before placing a call to Jenny. I couldn't wait to find out the big family secret.

"Hey, Liz. How are you?"

"OK. I just finished meeting with Bjorn. I can't say I learned anything new."

"Do you think he was involved in Aunt Peg's murder?"

"Probably not, but I haven't eliminated the possibility. So, spill, what's the big secret?" I asked.

"OK, so you know the Thomases and the Kelleys migrated over from Ireland together like eons ago, right?"

"Yeah?" I could hear the excitement in Jenny's voice.

"Turns out the long-ago Kelleys were pirates. They started their fortune from stolen money hidden away in baggage on the trip. My great uncle five times removed was drinking Irish whiskey with one of the Thomases and confessed. The Thomases have been holding it over the Kelleys ever since."

"Seriously? Why is that such a big deal? Sounds kind of romantic to me," I said.

"That's what I told Aunt Jane. You know how Charleston is though. There's new money and old money. And tainted old money is a whole other category."

"That's silly."

"Yeah. My generation is so not into all that. I convinced Aunt Jane we should call Grandpa Liam and tell him."

"Yikes, how did he take it?" I asked.

"He already knew. Turns out he had a plan all along in case word got out. Dad thinks it could be great marketing for the shipping company. He has an ad campaign ready to go. 'Ahoy Maties' and all that."

I chuckled. "Awesome work, Jenny. Any word on Jackson?"

"No. I've called all his friends. No one's seen him. Dad's sick with worry."

"My former boss is circulating Jackson's picture. I'll let you know as soon as I hear anything. I'm praying for you guys." I hoped that gave her some consolation.

"Thanks."

"I gotta run. I'm sitting in a pastry shop waiting on Lou, and he just walked in. I'll call you when I get back. Love you."

Lou waved Annalise off as she approached our table with a plate of pastries. Patting his tummy, he said, "Doll, you will make me fat. I couldn't possibly eat another one." Turning to me he said, "What did you think about Bjorn?"

"A little too smooth. And I sure didn't like the looks of those men who barged into the shop. I wish I'd had more time to talk to him. You cut that off."

He gave me a sheepish look. "Sorry."

"At least we've met. If I need to call him and follow up, it'll be easier."

Lou glanced at his phone. "Do you want to pop by the Louvre? We have time."

"Sure." Being surrounded by beautiful masterpieces of art sounded like a perfect antidote to the day. Annalise and I said our goodbyes, and I promised to call her when I knew more about Peg's murder.

Walking into the palace-like building of the Louvre, Lou wanted to start with the Egyptian collection. I was eager to see the statue of Venus de Milo, so we separated, agreeing to meet in front of the Mona Lisa in an hour. I was grateful for the solitude and some time to think. In minutes, my thoughts about the case faded as I was pulled into the beauty and the history of all the grand masterpieces. Sculptures, paintings, and antiquities in all forms and sizes.

Before I realized it, the hour had flown by, and I arrived fifteen minutes past our appointed meeting time.

"Sorry, I'm late. I completely lost track of time."

Lou was absorbed in the Mona Lisa. "She looks like she has some big secret, doesn't she? That smirk. How about you Liz, do you have any secrets? You already know mine."

I wasn't expecting that question. I dodged it by letting him in on the Kelley family secret.

"Oh, my God. Why didn't Peg tell me? If word gets out, it could hurt our business."

"I don't think she knew until recently." I filled him in on how I discovered there was a Kelley family secret to begin with. "Liam may go public with it. But it'll probably be a while. Just so you know."

"Damn. I guess I better think through how I'll handle that." He paused for a moment. "Liz, you didn't exactly answer my question. I asked if you had any secrets," he said pointing his finger at me.

"These aren't really secrets, but there are a couple of things you don't know about me." I sighed. "Let's move to a bench."

Lou reluctantly left the Mona Lisa. Once seated, I told him the details of my failed marriage, and my baby dying in utero. Lou wrapped his arm around my shoulder as a tear spilled down my cheek.

"Lizzie, I'm so sorry." We were silent for a few minutes as I struggled to regain my composure.

Lou broke the silence. "You OK?"

"Yeah." I rested my head on his shoulder.

"You said a few things—"

I blurted out. "I met a guy last night, and I'm kinda dating Brad."

"Get out—what? Who's the guy? And Brad! You are one lucky girl. When did that happen?"

I told him about J.P., Brad's kisses, and Peg's request in her letter.

"Details on those kisses, doll."

Blushing, I described the best kiss I'd ever had. "What should I do? J.P wants to see me again, but I feel like I'm being disloyal to Brad. Peg too."

"I've never met this J.P. guy but I'd say Brad, hands down. Relationships are hard. I just had to break one off."

"Sorry."

"Yeah. It was going nowhere. He's married."

"What's his name?"

"Joe." Ah, the mysterious boyfriend. "Are you OK about it?"

"I will be."

Patting his thigh, I asked, "What was in Peg's letter to you?"

"Advice on the business. Appreciation for our friendship and partnership. She encouraged me to keep up the acting. Said sometimes you just need to do things for your soul. She asked me to watch out for you. Course I was already doing that." Lou playfully poked me in the ribs. "What do you say we tie one on for our last night in Paris, Lizzie? We've earned it."

Lou and I went to a dance club in downtown Paris. Boy can Lou dance, and it sure felt good to let off some steam. We danced until the wee hours of the morning.

***

Tired from last night, I was grateful there'd be plenty of time to sleep on the flight back to Charleston. Lou was once again seated next to me in first class. I wondered if I'd be able to get any work done.

Once airborne, I lowered the tray and pulled out my index cards and notepad. What had I learned from the trip? Bjorn had money troubles. Bjorn was somehow involved with the Corsican Mafia. Bjorn had an alibi. Did Peg suspect his mafia connections? Everything I knew indicated that she tended to squelch any doubts concerning Bjorn. On the other hand, maybe a Mafia member suspected she knew something? That was possible. Bjorn was not in Peg's will, so money-wise he had more to gain by keeping her alive and eventually marrying her. Although there were no signs that either one of them was contemplating marriage.

I tapped Lou on the shoulder. He was also working, transcribing notes from clients into his laptop. Keeping my voice low, I said, "Did you mention to Peg that you suspected Bjorn had Corsican Mafia connections?"

"No. It was bad enough when I said I didn't trust him. To keep the peace, I kept my mouth shut after that."

"Were those guys who showed up at Bjorn's ever there when you guys were?" I asked.

"Yes. Peg was oblivious, busy inspecting various pieces of furniture we were interested in purchasing, but I had my antennae up. Do you think Bjorn had something to do with her murder?"

"Not sure. Just trying to put a few puzzle pieces together. Sorry to interrupt." I returned to my notes. Were there any outliers I missed? I turned on my laptop and opened my email, and transcribed some notes from Jenny's earlier email. I noticed that I was doing the opposite of Lou. Call me old-fashioned or tactile. Writing items down versus typing them into a computer was what worked for me. My inbox pinged with an email from Gunner.

> Liz,
>
> Negative on the fingerprints.
>
> Still trying to find Jackson. But while reviewing the videos from the night of Peg's murder, I stumbled on this. It's from the coffee shop across the street. Forward to 09:15. Looks like Jackson to me. What do you think? Let me know if you want me to poke around or if you want to do the legwork.
>
> Gunner

I shot a quick response back.

> Great work, Gunner. I'll follow up. I owe you a drink.

I was relieved Lou's prints weren't on the gun. Was Jackson somehow involved in Peg's murder? I hoped not. I reviewed all of my notes and considered the possibility. I'd missed a major point. If the murder was premeditated and set up by Alex or Bjorn, why use my gun? A contract killer would definitely use their own weapon. On the other hand, premeditated and my gun being the murder weapon pointed to me. J.P. and Gunner were right. I was a prime suspect. I had a motive—money of which I knew nothing about, but try proving that. I had the means. That damn gun. I had no alibi. And because I'd been at her home that night, my fingerprints were all over the place.

OK, I didn't do it. That I knew for sure. So what if the killing was random? It would be just like Jackson to show up at Peg's in the middle of the night and ask for money. Maybe he picked up the gun and it accidentally went off. I wondered if Sam bothered to check the juvenile records when he ran the fingerprints. If it was Jackson, it would be yet another blow to the Kelley family. I hoped my suspicions were wrong.

The flight attendant arrived with our meals. I'd ordered chicken glazed with a sweet honey barbeque sauce accompanied by green beans and sweet potato. Lou had opted for the steak. We chatted as we ate, each of us deliberately avoiding any subject involving Peg and her murder. After dessert, I selected a movie and put my headphones on. Thirty minutes later, I fell fast asleep.

Hours later, we walked off the plane to a lovely homecoming. Nothing better than being greeted by two cops. One of them was Sam, and he was grinning from ear to ear. I didn't recognize the other one. I wondered where Matt was.

Lou stopped mid-step and grabbed my arm. "Liz looks like they're headed for you."

Sam pulled out his cuffs. "Liz Adams, you're under arrest for the murder of Peg Kelley-Thomas."

Lou gasped, clutching at his stomach as if he had been sucker-punched.

The second cop proceeded to read me my Miranda rights while Sam cuffed me. Sam was enjoying this entirely too much. "Thought you could get away with sneaking out of the country, Lightweight Liz? Pleasure trip to Paris with your boyfriend? Ain't too worried about your best friend's murder, are you?"

Seriously, if he was any detective worth his salts, he'd know that Lou was gay. Lou had recovered from his initial shock and loudly protested, "She's trying to solve Peg's murder."

I wanted to put my fingers to my lips, but that was impossible, so I shushed him instead.

"Oh yeah? Sure would like to hear more about that. Be ready to come down to the station to make a statement." Sam pointed at Lou.

I was shocked to my core. I was on their side. Trying to help them solve the case. How would Liam and Camille react when they heard the news? My stomach churned with anxiety. I asked Lou to pick up my bag, my car, and take care of Duke. I also asked him to call Gunner and let him know what had happened. I needed Gunner to check on the other prints on my gun to determine if they matched Jackson's. Boy, I was going to owe both of them big time.

Lou walked off singing Bon Jovi's "Wanted Dead or Alive" under his breath.

***

My new lodging was quite the contrast to our Paris accommodations. Dressed in the latest orange fashion statement, I was escorted to a cell that consisted of a hard concrete floor, two beds with thin ticking mattresses, and sheets that felt like sandpaper, all accompanied by the lovely smell of urine and other body odors. I could hardly wait for my gourmet meal. I wanted to curl up in a ball and bawl my eyes out. My best friend was dead … worse than dead, murdered. I was supposed to be out there finding her killer. Instead, I was locked up and accused of being the perp. Self-pity threatened to engulf me. *Oh God, I sure need your help.*

If my world wasn't bleak enough, my cellmate had just arrived. I had a feeling orange wasn't her usual fashion statement either, but at least it was someone I knew.

Chapter 25

Sabrina was a beautiful, freckle-faced, young woman. She had hazel eyes and a short-cropped auburn pageboy that set off the angles of her face. Her large breasts stood at attention on her petite, athletic frame. Her profession was hooker, prostitute, or night lady, as Gunner liked to say.

"Well, my, my. What are you doing here, gal friend?"

"Hey, Sabrina, pull up a cot."

She sat opposite me. "Actually, I'm not surprised to find you in jail. Your face is plastered all over the news. Sorry about Peg. I bawled my mascara off when I heard she died."

"How come you're here? I thought Sammie had all of you covered?"

Sammie was Sabrina's boss, who just happened to be a seventy-year-old woman, extremely wealthy and very well-connected in Charleston. She contributed large sums to the police force and had top-notch attorneys on her side. She had quite the high-class clientele.

"I was brought in by some rookie." Sabrina rolled her eyes.

Most of the force knew better than to bring in Sammie's girls. It wasn't worth the hassle and the paperwork. They were usually back out in the length of time it took to make a phone call.

She continued, "Sammie went with Teresa to someplace in the Caribbean. She doesn't get back until Sunday."

Teresa was her successor. As I said, Sammie had quite the operation, including a succession plan. She treated her employees well.

"Soooooo, did you do it?" Sabrina asked.

"Do what?"

"Did you kill Peg?"

"Are you kidding? No. I've been working my butt off trying to find out who did."

"Heard you're getting a lot of money from Peg. So, what's the 411?" Sabrina shifted her weight on the mattress and waited for my response.

My mind started spinning. A lot of money. How was that word out already? I remembered Gunner mentioning Sabrina's name from the surveillance tapes. Maybe she saw something that night.

"Girl … what's going on in that head of yours?" she asked.

"The 411 is I didn't do it. Maybe her ex, Alex. Up to his ears in debt, he threatened Peg if she didn't give him more money. Problem is, he has an airtight alibi, and he wasn't in the will. There's Lou, her business partner, but I just can't see that one. Her sister, Chantal, was insanely jealous of her. And Peg had a boyfriend, Bjorn who lives in Paris and may or may not have ties to the Corsican mafia. I just returned from there. The cops nabbed me at the airport." I groaned in frustration. "Then there's Jackson, her drug-addicted nephew. Maybe he hit her up for money and it got out of hand." Ugh. I needed to be out there working the case instead of locked up in here. I wished I had my phone so I could show her a picture of Jackson. Damn Sam.

"Sabrina, have you seen anything, heard anything that might help? Any rumors running on the street?"

"There's a lot of talk about you. Some people think you were the heartless bitch who offed her best friend so she could inherit a fortune. Others think it was most likely that jerk, Alex. I haven't heard any talk about a boyfriend. By the way, I'm in the Alex camp. You know he's one of Sammie's clients, right? I won't touch him, but some of the other girls … well … and I've heard he has a temper."

"I didn't know he was one of Sammie's, but I'm not surprised."

"Haven't heard any rumors 'bout Lou and Chantal. Well, plenty of rumors about Chantal, but not around Peg's murder. But that's just Sabrina talkin'. Oh shit." Sabrina jumped up and covered her face with her hands.

"Whhhhaaaatt?" I squealed hoping she didn't just see a rat.

"Tina. I've been feeding her every night. You know. The homeless girl. She's in a bad state. Won't come out of this warehouse she's been holed up in. She's been like this before, but it's way worse than usual. Who'll feed her tonight?"

"I've been searching for Tina. Her folks haven't heard from her in weeks. Where is she?"

"The abandoned warehouse on Canal Street. I saw Tina the night Peg was killed. She was really restless. We sat under the bridge and talked for a spell. She said she might go see Peg. Maybe spend the night with her. She did that sometimes, ya' know. Well of course you do. Tina loved your friend Peg. She was always talking big 'bout her. A few hours after Tina wandered off I heard the sirens. I didn't think twice 'bout it. What the hell, sirens in Charleston ain't that uncommon."

My heart rate started to come down as Sabrina continued, "The next day I heard about Peg. Man, was I sad. Then I started looking for Tina. I wanted to tell her about Peg myself. I found her by accident when I was looking for a spot to conduct some business. Ditched that client when I found her holed up in that warehouse shivering and scared. She wouldn't talk to me, but I've been trying to help her ever since."

"Oh my gosh, I need to get ahold of Lou. Maybe he can help her." I hollered for the guard on duty.

"I need to make a phone call. Please, it's urgent."

The female guard studied my face and nodded. "I'll see what I can do."

A few minutes later she returned and unlocked the cell. "Come with me."

I followed her to the phone area, choosing the first device available on the mustard-colored wall. I still had my one free call.

"You have five minutes." Leaning against the wall, she watched as I punched in Lou's number.

As soon as he picked up, I got to the point. "I know where Tina is. I need for you to go see her. Take Cassie with you. It's urgent."

"OK. What's up?"

"I'm worried about her. My cellmate said she's not doing well." I didn't mention to listening ears that she might know something about Peg's murder. I gave him the address for the warehouse.

"Who's the cellmate?"

"Long story. Please go soon."

"I'm on it, doll."

"Thank you. How's Duke?"

"He's great. He was disappointed to see me versus you. By the way, congratulations, you made national news. Your parents called me, worried."

I winced. "They're not on the way, are they?"

"I convinced them to wait until after your bail hearing," he replied. "Hanging with you is a real adventure."

"Yeah, I know. I promise I'll make it up to you."

The guard guided me back to the cell and turned the lock. Once inside, I began pacing back and forth, my nerves a jumbled mess. Sabrina begged me to stop. I couldn't sit down. I needed to be there with Lou. I was exploding with the questions I wanted to ask Tina. After what seemed like weeks, but in reality was only a few hours, Matt showed up.

"Liz, you're free to go." He unlocked the cell. "Lou's waiting for you."

"No way," Sabrina exclaimed. "She's not leaving until I hear what happened. I helped you find Tina. You gotta tell me how she is."

Matt considered for a long moment and then sighed. "Tina is fine. Liz's neighbors brought her down to the station. She confessed to shooting Peg. It was an accident. She picked up the gun just to look at it, and it went off."

"Oh my God!" Sabrina and I said in unison. I buried my face in my hands. How awful.

"What will happen to her?" Sabrina asked.

"We've contacted her parents. We're working on it. She'll be OK." Matt reassured the both of us.

On the ride home, Lou described what happened when they found Tina. She was huddled under blankets in a corner of the warehouse. When Cassie and Lou entered, she screamed. They both stopped in their tracks, afraid she'd bolt. After a few moments, Cassie walked over and sat next to her. Tina began sobbing, repeating, "I'm so sorry. I didn't mean it." Slowly, they drew the story out of her.

The heavy mist and humidity had caused Tina to seek another spot to sleep that night. She was tired and thirsty. She stopped by Peg's to ask if she could stay the night. Peg let her in, and then went to the kitchen to get a glass of water. The gun laid on the coffee table where I'd placed it when I left. Tina picked it up, curious. When Peg returned, she startled her. Tina whirled, swinging the gun in Peg's direction and it went off. Frightened, Tina dropped the weapon, bolted out the door, and ran to the warehouse where she'd been ever since that fateful night.

∗∗

And just like that, it was over. Back home, dressed in my robe and slippers, I snuggled up with Duke on the couch. TV headlines flashed across the local news.

> Charleston Private Investigator cleared of murder.
> Mentally ill homeless woman confesses to shooting local socialite and philanthropist, Peg Kelley-Thomas.

I hit the off button on the remote. I couldn't stand to watch any longer. It was all so tragic. And I couldn't shake the feeling that it was somehow my fault. When I'd voiced my guilty conscience to Lou, he tried to reassure me by stressing that it was an accident, and Tina might finally get the help she needed. She would most likely be committed to a mental institution. He'd said he bet Peg was smiling from heaven over that news. I found little solace or comfort in his words.

J.P. called the day after the news broke to congratulate me and update me on the investigation into Bjorn. Turns out that CM Partners aided in laundering drug money for the Corsican mafia. After J.P. confronted him, Bjorn agreed to rat out the mafia in exchange for a lighter sentence and protection for his family. J.P. was headed to the Caribbean in two weeks to investigate yet another money laundering case tied to the Corsican mafia. He asked if I wanted to join him. All expenses paid. I politely declined giving him the "I need time. Let's be friends" speech. He said he understood but the tone in his voice reflected disappointment.

Gunner did find out that Sam never checked the juvie records for prints, but it was a moot point. However, he did some additional investigating and found Jackson, who was now at a halfway house and actively working on his sobriety. Gunner and I were having drinks tonight to celebrate the case being solved.

I met Liam and Camille for dinner last night. They both thanked me for all of my work. Liam said they were rolling out the new ad campaign next month. He called Thomas Sr. and chewed him out over Alex's threats. Camille said Chantal was in a rehab facility for the next twelve months. The family would be able to visit her in three months. I looked up the place online. Chantal didn't seem to be roughing it.

When the news broke about my arrest, Brad called Lou, worried about me. After calling my parents to ease their concerns, I called Brad, and we'd spoken every day since then. We finalized the plans for my trip to California. He was sending a private plane for my visit. And, of course, Duke was welcome.

Jenny and I scheduled our Friday lunch, and our community was getting together next Sunday for a barbeque at Lou's place. Cassie broke it off with Sam once she found out he was the one who arrested me. Gwen was somewhat less nervous about being home alone.

It was over. Life was back to normal. Sort of.

I had a big hole in my heart, and I didn't feel at peace. Peg had been my best friend. I told her everything. That she'd kept secrets from me still stung. Time to visit her gravesite and clear the air.

I packed a bottle of merlot and a wine glass, grabbed a folding chair and slipped them into the trunk of my car. Putting the top down on the convertible, I let the wind soothe my frazzled nerves. Duke's tongue lopped to the side and his ears flapped in the wind.

It took me a few minutes to find Peg's gravesite. Setting the folding chair under the oak tree next to her marker, I uncorked the wine and poured a glass. Duke chased the birds against the backdrop of a setting sun while I sipped my wine.

While the sun cast pink and orange hues on cotton candy clouds, I spoke to her. "I'm sorry I didn't stay the night with you. Maybe it wouldn't have happened if the two of us were there. And I'm sorry about the gun. I never should have left it with you." Guilt consumed me, forming the lump of a sob in my throat. I placed my head in my hands and let the tears flow. As dusk settled in, I found my voice again. "You hurt my feelings, Peg. Why didn't you tell me your secrets? Why didn't you let me be there for you like you were there for me? I thought I was your closest friend. The person you'd share everything with. The good and the bad."

Anger flared as I recalled the frantic attempt to assuage my guilt, while trying to save my lily-white ass from being charged with murder. I flung the wine glass across the cemetery and watched it hit an oak tree and shatter into a million pieces. Maybe in time, I'd find some peace. The sense of betrayal from Peg's protected privacy was not the only source of my frustration. I didn't know how to digest the seeming senselessness of her death. The odd set of circumstances and events that aligned and ended her beautiful life. Knowing her secrets and the truth about her death made acceptance more difficult. Peg's life ended in the hands of someone afflicted by mental illness; a killer tormented by her own demons.

I had no place to direct my anger, the tip of the well of grief inside me. I'd been on a roller coaster of emotions, and I had a feeling the ride wasn't over. What had Peg been thinking leaving me all that money? Why didn't she tell me? The money and her loss left me with a lot to process.

Duke stopped chasing the seagulls and curled up next to my chair. I felt a cooling in the breeze and a buzzing in the air. In front of me, a hummingbird hovered for a minute and then flew off, leaving me wondering if it was ever there. The words "Let Go" rumbled from deep inside my chest, and I knew it was time to release the guilt that had consumed me while I unraveled the mystery of Peg's death. Perhaps she was speaking to me from the other side. Her death shook my belief in logic, reason, and everything requiring an explanation. Anything was possible. Life couldn't be reduced to flowcharts and index cards.

I raised the bottle of merlot to the sky and took one last swallow directly from the bottle. Then I poured the rest on her grave. To you, Peg. To your life and our friendship. I picked up the chair and whistled for Duke, taking one last gaze at Peg's headstone before heading home.

"Oh, Peg," I sighed, my heart aching, "I miss you so much."

Acknowledgments

My mission is to deliver a good story to the reader and benefit a larger community. A portion of the proceeds from this book will be donated to National Alliance for the Mentally Ill, NAMI. I hope you enjoyed the story.

First, thanks to God. Without faith, the making of this book would have been impossible. A big thank you to my readers.

It indeed takes a village to create a book. Thank you to all who supported me along the way, especially my greatest cheerleader, my husband. Thank you also to my parents, our son, my beta readers, my author and artist friends, my cover designer, my aqua fit helpers, our extended family and friends, my coaches, and editors. A shout out to each of our beloved Labs who influenced Duke's character.

Keep turning the page for Liz's recipes and a sneak peek at Carmel Conundrum. Please visit my website for additional recipes and news.

All the best,

Stacy Wilder
www.storystacy.com

Liz's King Ranch Chicken

Ingredients:

1 can cream of mushroom soup
1 can cream of chicken soup
1 can Rotel tomatoes
1 cup chicken stock
rotisserie chicken
9x12 baking dish

8 oz. (2 cups) cheddar cheese
1 package corn tortillas
1 white onion diced
1 green bell pepper diced
1 Tsp ancho chili powder
½ tsp garlic salt Pepper
to taste

Preheat oven to 375 degrees.

Place corn tortillas in a bowl and cover with chicken stock. Soak until soft.

Shred chicken. Fine dice onion and bell pepper. Combine soup and cheese in a separate bowl. Use half of the tortillas to cover the bottom of the baking dish. Layer half of the chicken on top followed by half of the onion and green pepper. Follow with half of the cheese/soup mixture. Repeat. Pour can of Rotel on top.

Bake for thirty minutes.

Enjoy!

Charleston Conundrum Cookies

This recipe is compliments of Chef Amber Griffin, Vermont. Chef Amber baked these during When Words Count Pitch Week Competition XXI. She is an amazing chef. Thank you Amber for allowing me to share this recipe.

Ingredients:

2 sticks butter (softened)
1 cup brown sugar
1 cup white sugar
1/2 teaspoon salt
2 eggs
1/2 bag shredded coconut
1/2 bag heath bar bits

1 cup chocolate chips
3/4 cup pepita seeds
1 teaspoon vanilla
2 cups flour
1 teaspoon baking soda
1/2 bag Lays potato chips (crushed)

Preheat oven to 350 degrees. Cream butter, sugar, and salt together. Add the eggs and vanilla. Mix well. Add flour and baking soda. Mix well. Add coconut, Heath bits, chocolate chips, and pepita seeds.

Mix until just combined. Stir in crushed potato chips. Drop on a baking sheet and bake for twelve to fifteen minutes. Makes approximately forty-eight cookies.

Enjoy!

Lou's Favorite Egg Salad

Ingredients:

eight hard-boiled eggs
¼ cup mayonnaise
2 Tsp. Dijon mustard
4 Tsp. finely chopped celery (about 2 stalks)
4 Tsp. finely chopped red onion
1 Tsp. dill
garlic salt to taste
pepper to taste
¼ tsp. smoked paprika
fresh dill as garnish

Finely chop the eggs, celery, and red onion and place them in a bowl. Stir in mayo, mustard, dill, garlic salt pepper, and paprika. Garnish with fresh dill. Serve on your favorite bread. Enjoy!

Liz's Oops Salad

Ingredients:

1 bag of mixed spring greens
I cup of strawberries diced
A few handfuls of blueberries
A few handfuls of raspberries
A few handfuls of blackberries

Wash and dry fresh produce. Toss and serve with your favorite raspberry vinaigrette. Garnish with toasted almonds.

The Charleston Conundrum Playlist:

1. "Fire and Rain," James Taylor
2. "Dancing Queen," ABBA
3. "S.O.S.," ABBA
4. "I Heard It Through the Grapevine," Marvin Gaye
5. "I Second That Emotion," The Miracles
6. "If I Could Turn Back Time," Cher
7. "If I Were a Rich Man," Robert Merrill's version
8. "Hello," Adele
9. "Edge of Glory," Lady Gaga
10. "Wanted Dead Or Alive," Bon Jovi

A sneak peek at….*Carmel Conundrum*

Duke and I stepped off the private jet and walked across the tarmac to climb into a waiting limousine. I could definitely get used to this lifestyle. The flight had been smooth, the steward attentive and friendly. Brad had thought of all the details, including rawhides on the plane for Duke and a lobster lunch for me. Duke, my six-year-old black Labrador, acted as if he had been flying private all his life. I was both nervous and excited to see Brad. Our mutual friend, Peg, had encouraged both of us to stay in touch in a letter she left for each of us after her death. I was here to visit him, check out a piece of property she'd left me, and take a break from the PI business.

Once things had settled down after Peg's murder, Brad and I had planned this trip, and we'd been communicating daily. My heart ached over the loss of my best friend, and I was still recovering from trying to solve her murder and being accused of it at the same time. Sharing the grief with Peg's childhood friend, Brad, and her business partner and dear friend, Lou, had helped.

I still wasn't sure what category Brad fell into for me. Certainly friend. Possible lover. Maybe more. Before leaving Charleston, I'd changed outfits three times, eventually deciding on a simple white peasant blouse, jeans, and a pair of sexy sling-back sandals. So far, Brad and I had only exchanged a kiss—and oh, that kiss—and some suggestive phone conversations.

Brad had a business meeting that couldn't be rescheduled so he sent the car instead. Duke, oblivious to my nerves, hung his head out the limousine window, tongue flopping. His nose wiggled, taking in the smells of California. The cool dry breeze was refreshing. What a change in climate from Charleston.

As we pulled into the driveway, I was awestruck by Brad's home, a gray stone two-story right on the Pacific. The property alone had to be worth a mint. A Southern-style wrap-around driftwood porch framed the front. I spotted him sitting in an Adirondack chair waiting. He hopped up and jumped down the stairs as soon as we pulled into the circular driveway in front.

"Liz. Duke! I'm sorry I couldn't meet you at the airport."

I felt disappointed and a bit jealous when he gave me a rather chaste kiss and took Duke's leash lavishing love on him. The limo driver placed my luggage inside the house and Brad sent him on his way.

"I'll take Duke for a quick walk so he can do his business. You go on inside and make yourself at home. The powder room is on the left, right off the entry."

Walking inside I took in the view. Large glass windows framed the Pacific Ocean. Today the waves were choppy. The sun drifted in and out of long white clouds, casting shadows on the water. Further back from the house were a large outdoor kitchen and an infinity pool. Nice.

As soon as I finished freshening up, Brad and Duke walked in, and my heart did a flip-flop. Brad sported a white polo, untucked, and navy shorts. The white showcased his golden California tan.

"Liz." He reached for me, wrapping me in those well-toned arms, and kissed me slow, tender, and deep. Nothing chaste about this kiss. Boldly, I slipped my hands underneath his shirt relishing the warmth of his smooth skin. Ignorant of the heat building between the two of us, Duke curled up by the fireplace and settled in for a nap. I stepped back before things spiraled out of hand.

Brad sighed and ran his fingers through his hair. "Let me show you your room so you can get settled."

The guest bedroom was layered in shades of gray accented with pops of aquamarine. The bed was stacked with pillows and looked inviting. Covering a yawn with my hand, I let out a big sigh.

"Why don't you take a nap? I'm sure you're exhausted."

"Actually, that sounds great. You don't mind?"

He gave me another long kiss as an answer. "Sweet dreams."

Two hours later, I awakened. Sitting up in the bed, I surveyed my surroundings. The artwork was a bit modern for my taste, abstracts reflecting identical hues of gray and blue. Several remotes sat on the bedside table. One was for the shades.

Raising them, I was greeted with an amazing view of the ocean. I lowered them back down and picked up the TV remote. I was curious because I didn't see a TV in the room. As I pressed the 'on' button, a painting hanging over the long dresser, where my suitcase sat, changed into a baseball game. Way cool.

I pulled my cosmetic case out of my suitcase and headed for the bathroom to brush my teeth. The bathroom had gray slate floors and an amazing whirlpool tub. The shower had two large showerheads. The countertops were a light gray granite. There was even artwork in the bathroom. Peg had been a high-end decorator before she passed. I bet she'd helped him decorate this place.

I found Brad in the kitchen chopping vegetables while listening to the Eagles, Duke curled at his feet.

"Hey, gorgeous. How'd you sleep?"

"Great. I can't believe I slept for two hours."

"You probably needed it. I'm so glad you are here." Setting down the knife, he walked over and kissed me.

I blushed suddenly feeling awkward and a bit shy. Duke finally realized I was in the room and wiggled toward me, tail wagging. I nodded at the chopped veggies. "Um, can I help?"

"Sure. Pick a bottle of wine from the wine fridge. It's in the pantry. I thought we'd eat in tonight. I'm barbequing steaks."

After perusing the wine selection, I chose a shiraz. I twisted the cap off and poured each of us a glass. "Did Peg help you decorate this place? Your home is gorgeous."

"Of course she did. You think I could do this by myself?" He chuckled.

His phone buzzed. Glancing at the name on the screen, he said, "Sorry. I've got to take this call."

I couldn't help overhearing Brad's side of the conversation.

"Hey, Tim, what's up? No way. Who reported it this time?" He paused a moment to listen, then said, "We need to get to the bottom of this. Soon. Before word gets out and our reputation is destroyed." Glancing over at me, he continued, "I have an idea. Check my calendar and book a meeting for Monday, preferably morning. We can discuss what I have in mind then."

Brad turned back toward me. "I have a business proposition for you."

www.ingramcontent.com/pod-product-compliance
Lightning Source LLC
Chambersburg PA
CBHW020022310726
48970CB00007B/2162